THE CASE
OF
Malena Merian

The Case of
Malena Merian

Malena Merian

XULON PRESS ELITE

Xulon Press Elite
2301 Lucien Way #415
Maitland, FL 32751
407.339.4217
www.xulonpress.com

© 2021 by Malena Merian

All rights reserved solely by the author. The author guarantees all contents are original and do not infringe upon the legal rights of any other person or work. No part of this book may be reproduced in any form without the permission of the author. The views expressed in this book are not necessarily those of the publisher.

Due to the changing nature of the Internet, if there are any web addresses, links, or URLs included in this manuscript, these may have been altered and may no longer be accessible. The views and opinions shared in this book belong solely to the author and do not necessarily reflect those of the publisher. The publisher therefore disclaims responsibility for the views or opinions expressed within the work.

Unless otherwise indicated, Scripture quotations taken from the New King James Version (NKJV). Copyright © 1982 by Thomas Nelson, Inc. Used by permission. All rights reserved.

Edited by Xulon Press.

Paperback ISBN-13: 978-1-66283-077-8
Ebook ISBN-13: 978-1-66283-078-5

Table of Contents

Dedication vii

Chapter 1: The Possession. 1
Chapter 2: Demon Possession. 35
Chapter 3: The Devil is a Real Persona 39
Chapter 4: My Conversion Story 47
Chapter 5: The Lord's church,
    the Church of Christ. 54
Chapter 6: The New Age Movement 67
Chapter 7: Yoga 84
Chapter 8: Occultism 89
Chapter 9: Law of Attraction (Manifesting) 99
Chapter 10: Astrology 108
Chapter 11: Séances and
    Communicating with the Dead. 114
Chapter 12: Harry Potter. 118
Chapter 13: Conclusion and Poem 125

Works Cited. 130

Dedication

To my parents and brethren around the world and to all the souls searching for truth and genuine love and salvation, only found in Jesus Christ.
Amen.

Jesus says:

> John 10:10
> "The thief does not come except to steal, and to kill, and to destroy. I have come that they may have life, and that they may have *it* more abundantly."

> Matthew 11:28-30
> "Come to Me, all you who labor and are heavy laden, and I will give you rest. Take My yoke upon you and learn from Me, for I am gentle and lowly in heart, and you will find rest for your souls. For My yoke is easy and My burden is light."

Dear Reader,

This is my real story.
    I was born into a non-practicing Catholic family. The Bible used to be on the top of a shelf full of dust. My mother is from the Dominican Republic and my father from Italy, but I was raised in Switzerland. I am an only child. My early years were happy years, covered with an abundance of love and attention. During school holidays, we would often travel to the Dominican Republic and Italy for leisure. At school, I was a rather popular student and had a lot of friends and acquaintances.
    At the age of sixteen, we moved to the Dominican Republic. We stayed there for four years. I learned to drive a car there and I studied International Studies at University. At the age of twenty, we moved back to Switzerland where I was fed up with studying and decided to work for a multinational company in administration. Eventually, I started working for many different multinational companies. It felt great to be able to execute a diverse range of jobs without having studied any career in those jobs. At the age of twenty-eight and with a lot of experience, I started my study course in Switzerland and completed my degree in business administration. Finally, I had a degree to show to my employers, so that I could be

paid accordingly. My life before Christ was a monetarily good life, but it was dull. It was a life of working and travelling, sometimes alone, through Europe. I had a few good friends and maintained a strong bond with my family in the Dominican Republic. My dream had always been to live and work in the Dominican Republic, but it never came to fruition, so I stayed in Switzerland. Then 2016 came. It was a turbulent year. After having experienced a painful conversion, today, my passion is Christ and to spread the Gospel which is the good news of salvation to the world.

This book is intended to be a blessing to those seeking the truth and eternal life. As you may know, the soul is an eternal being and we only have two options, either we obey the Gospel of Christ and remain faithful until death going to Heaven to be with Jesus and the saints. Or we keep on with our vain life on earth, disobeying the Gospel of Christ resulting in eternally suffering in hell with the devil and his demons. Heaven and Hell are as real as earth. You ought to choose well in this life, as it will determine where you spend eternity.

I hope this book helps you to choose well and wisely the path of eternal salvation leading you to Christ and eternal life. In addition, I hope to provide insight into New Age and the dangers involved in it. My experience in New Age happened unbeknown to me. It was the result of the blind leading the blind and both fell into a ditch. In the Bible, in Luke 6:39 it says, "And He (Jesus) spoke a parable to them: Can the blind lead the blind? Will they not both fall into the ditch?" My fall was huge and painfully significant. I am here to tell you about my story of how I fell into the ditch of New Age. My short but powerful book will give you a deeper insight into the truth.

May God bless you abundantly and lead you to the road of eternal salvation.

To God be the Glory!

Chapter 1:

The Possession

It's the year 2016.

The year 2016 was a turbulent year. I remember being fed-up working in a big multinational company where I was an assistant to a female boss. I had just learned about another foul trick of hers. I was committed to end my temporary contract soon, although I was offered an extension, but I didn't want to work for such a character anymore. I decided to give up, so I quit that job and stayed at home sleeping and reading literature. Sometimes, I would write poetry, raw poetry. I had experienced enough at that company for almost a year that I had plenty of things to write. The poem I wrote about my female boss was called Inferno.

Inferno

there's nothing better,
than a piece of paper
and a pen.
here,
writing it all down

peng! peng! peng!
Yet an artillery of words
can't fix up the hurt
cut
the spreading of ache
keeps me from so many ings
especially sleep-
ing
no peace I find,
only stress and
sound around
now crying
once again
on the wet, cold,
ground
this the end,
to a horrific event;
you'll see,
it will all make sense-
I just don't care
for anyone's non- or consents,
all I want is to rest,
and get back to content!
no more,
apocalyptic bitch,
hell no!
go back to inferno.

    Who would have known that I myself would experience a real inferno by the end of that year?

The First Move

I was looking for a quiet apartment in a rural village. I wanted to be far away from the noise of the city. I had chosen the wrong apartment earlier. I had moved in during holiday season, so it was very quiet but as soon as vacation time was over and the tenants returned, I learned it was a building with lots of babies and toddlers. I love children, but I heard non-stop noise in my bedroom at very late hours and could not sleep. I just wanted to sleep, as I needed to work the next day. Having had that experience, I was now eager to find myself a new, quiet home. This time without toddlers living directly above me. I kept searching every day on the internet for the perfect apartment. About two weeks later, I found one. It was a modern one, light flooded, heated wooden floors, a fully equipped bathroom with a washing machine and dryer, a small walk-in closet and a terrace with teak flooring displaying a fantastic view into vineyards. It was designed by an architect who won a world-renowned prize. What a beautiful view! I immediately contacted the owner for a viewing appointment, however, he said he would not be in the village until two weeks' time. I thought to myself, "Well, somebody is in no rush to rent the apartment out"! Later I found out that the owner was listed amongst the richest people in Switzerland. Nevertheless, I waited, and after two weeks I was able to see the long-desired apartment. I had already gone up there once to see it from the outside and I liked it very much. It was very tranquil, and the colors of spring were mind-blowingly beautiful. I felt at peace up there close to the woods. I felt at home as I heard the pure raw sounds of nature clearly in my ears. All of this conveyed to me a real sense of peace, of coming home. I knew I was one of the first interested parties and my chances of getting the apartment were good. I dreamily went off in my car to buy some groceries.

The Second Move and the Apartment in the Woods

The day I signed the contract for the apartment finally came. I was overjoyed that I had found myself a nice and decent apartment in a rather posh village. I took the contract to the post office, registered it, and off it went! Because they were doing some minor renovations on the apartment, I had to wait two more weeks before the apartment was mine. On move in day, I remember that I had no bed frame because I had sold all my furniture to the new tenant of my past apartment, and so I moved in with just one big mattress on the heated floor. I wanted to feel the warmth of the floor, so I kept sleeping like that for the rest of my stay there.

As excited as I was to be in my apartment, sleeping there soon became an unexpected issue. It started the first night I slept there. I just could not fall asleep. In the beginning, I thought it was because of the euphoria I felt for my new apartment. I had some valerian pills, which I had never used before, so I decided to try them out to see if they would work. They are supposed to help with insomnia. Unfortunately, I still could not sleep. I put on some Chopin to see if I would eventually doze off, but nothing happened until around 4:00 am. When the birds were waking up and singing outside, that is when I could fall asleep. Can you imagine every night this same sleeping pattern? Since I was unemployed at that time, this did not affect my daytime routine. I would sleep until noon, but I was worried what would happen if I had to go back to work. Would I need to feed myself sleeping pills? I did not want that.

This state of poor sleeping pressed on for more than two weeks. I finally decided to sleep at my mother's house where I found I could sleep well again. Thus, started my new routine. I would sleep at my mother's house at night and during the day, stay in my apartment. Then every night I would drive back to my mother's house to sleep. Since we were close, she didn't mind having me over to sleep in my bedroom and then commute daily back and forth to the apartment. I did not want to give up, for a second time, an apartment that I loved and had gotten for myself. But I just could not figure out why I could not sleep in my apartment and my mother felt strange about it as well. She could not understand why I had such a difficult time sleeping there, since it was a perfect place for me.

During my unemployment, I had the chance to travel on weekends to Italy and the southern part of Switzerland. This spiced up my boring Monday through Friday. Sometimes, I would go on these blissful adventures with my mom. I saw beautiful scenery, ate fantastic food (I am a gourmand), and life was just great! I was in no hurry to get back to work after the catastrophic last experience I had, but Fall came, I was getting bored of travelling during weekends. I started searching more intensely for suitable employment. Lo and behold, I found a very good one, but it was more than one hour away from home in a beautiful city in Switzerland. If I took the job, I would have to commute each day around three hours (traffic included) for me to reach my destination on time! That was just too much of a waste of time spent on the highways. I was a bit sad at the thought of leaving this apartment, but at this stage I had not yet had the interview, only an invitation to come to the interview. From the invitation, I could tell the interview would be with a woman! My possible future boss would be a woman again!? My euphoria died at that thought and I wasn't really happy to go to the interview anymore, but I wanted it to give it a try! Filled with optimism, I went on the journey to this beautiful city. I met a professional woman in her late forties. She was demanding, but polite. I just kept on thinking how she would be after the interview if I worked for her. Would she metamorphose into a devil as my previous boss had? I was very concerned about it but did not want her to notice. She told me after our interview that she wanted to hire me. I was flattered but told her I would need to think carefully about it. We said goodbye and I drove back home through valleys full of green pastures, sheep, and cows. Picturesque indeed!

Arriving home, I thought, *"You know, I don't want to say goodbye to this wonderful place even though it's unable to give me the rest that I need."* I thought of this new challenging role, but also of how I would lose my wonderful apartment right near the woods. I felt the need to have and keep this apartment so overwhelming almost obsessing about it. I didn't tell my parents because I wanted to make up my own mind. Eventually, I called the recruiter regarding the open job position and told him that I was sorry, but I did not want to take the position. All sorts of scenarios came to my mind in the following days when I considered working for a woman again. I didn't want to risk being bullied again.

By November, I was so fed up with my sleeping situation I just wanted to know why I could not fall asleep just like everybody else in that building would. There must be a reason. Maybe something was wrong energetically? I was tired of sleeping at my mother's house. Looking for answers, I thought I would address my problem with my friends from then on. I decided that I would ask a friend Marla who was a cosmetics lady and Jim, an ex-coworker from the multinational company, what to do in such cases. Marla told me immediately that it was not a good sign at all. She thought that I needed to move out. She, like my mother, did not have a good feeling at all. Jim, who was into all sorts of New Age, and told me he could talk to angels, said to me that I had house ghosts who needed to be put away through a shamanic ritual. Since I still did not want to move out of that place, I opted for plan b, to have a shamanic ritual done.

For your understanding, back then, I was a weekend Catholic who believed in Jesus and God but had never read one page of the Bible for myself. My understanding of Christianity and following Jesus was limited. I felt that I was a sinner, so I never went up to take the altar bread for communion. I just listened to the sermon and prayed. I thought the devil and his demons were an invention of Hollywood. Such was the narrowness of my understanding. I would soon learn that I was very far from reality. Very, very far from reality.

Why Had I Listened to Jim?

I had listened to my friend Jim because we had a casual but solid friendship. He was into communication, and he had helped me with my letter writing in English, and my job application went under his sharp eye in the past. I had trust in him. It was my understanding that Jim was into New Age as he told me that he spoke to angels. I could not really believe that he actually spoke to angels, but it didn't ring any alarm bells in my mind either. Everyone has certain things they do to feel better about situations or ways to deal with stress. Maybe talking to "angels" was his. So, I told him about my apartment and sleep situation. I told him everything about how I could not find rest in my apartment during the evening and night hours and how as soon as I would hear the early birds in the morning, I would fall asleep. That is when he told me about cleansing my apartment from house spirits. I was desperate to sleep, and my curiosity was peaked. I wondered what house spirits were all about. I had never really heard of house spirits before. Maybe in Hollywood movies. But here? Never.

Jim suggested to me a book by a self-claimed shaman dressed all in white. I am not going to mention the name of the shaman, but bear in mind that there are thousands and thousands of shamans and witches who sell their occult products on the internet. I felt a bit hesitant at first, because she was a witch and I remember from school days, that witches were burned at the stake in the Middle Ages. Eventually, I told him to tell me the name of the book.

I immediately bought it on iTunes, and I read the table of contents I learned that she had all types of "recipes" of what to do in which situation. I went straight to "what to do if you have house spirits in your home." I read it many times before getting into action. I read her story about when she was little and how she would hear things move in her kitchen. Her grandparents, being witches too, would calm the noise by some incomprehensible phrases and rituals. When I read that, I could not quite believe it. All this incense, and abraca-whatever could actually bring my sleep back? Since I am a problem-solving person who does not give up easily and I needed sleep and peace, I thought that it was worth a try. I didn't believe in evil spirits or angels or shamans or even house spirits really, but I was willing to try anything. I went, as a Catholic, to a souvenir shop of a Catholic Basilica and bought all the necessary ingredients to cleanse my apartment of house spirits. The list was very long. It included items like incense, candles, oil from grapes etc.

Here is the poem I wrote before the ritual. Little did I know that it would foreshadow things to come:

Corpse
Whenever my eyes see
an animal corpse
on the street
my soul creeps out
holds a prayer out loud
Your mother
father, son,
your daughter,
friend, lover
is not returning home
ever after
do not wait-
Please,
it was a human
running late
running
late
The reaction,
too late.
it's nice to have brakes
for God's sake!
time-
a running gag.

The Ritual

> 1 Peter 5:8 says, "Be sober, be vigilant; because your adversary the devil walks about like a roaring lion, seeking whom he may devour."

On a cloudy evening in the beginning of December, I started the ritual. I was committed to fight these house spirits and get my sleep back with the ritual. I lit the candles and waved the incense around the house while repeating a kind of prayer about cleansing the spirits that I couldn't understand. In a short time, my apartment was filled with pure incense smoke and I could not see anything. This forced me to open the windows so that some oxygen could enter. I coughed several times and went to the kitchen. It was there I had placed, four apple seeds, which had not yet been ingested, as the book told me to have ready. I quickly took them into my hand, put them in my mouth, and drank some water. Then I went out to the front of the apartment to get the four remaining seeds as instructed and buried them outside my home while waiting for the smoke to dissipate. On that evening I was sure I would sleep well. After all this time and all the preparation and now performing the ritual, I was convinced that I would definitely sleep well again.

A Strange Presence

After the ritual, I took a walk through the valley where I lived, and I perceived a strange presence following me very closely. I cannot describe it in words, but I felt that I was not alone anymore, as if an unseen shadow was following me. As I was feeling this presence, I decided I would write to my friend Jim, and ask him about the things that were happening to me. He answered me saying that *this was my protective angel* and that I should not be afraid. Though the thought of a protective angel should bring comfort and peace, I remember very well that night the nightmares began. I had never had such horrible nightmares. I began to see frightening monstrous creatures that I prefer not to remember.

In one nightmare, I saw an audience in the yoga sitting position with white garments and I was in the crowd. In front of us were three masters. Suddenly, I saw how the three masters were illuminated and staring with black eyes at me as they were seeing a picture of me on the pedestal. I woke up in utter fear and I understood that something evil was behind me.

In another significant nightmare, I saw a giant Aries, the diabolic symbol of Satan as a goat. He had a black face, black feet, and black horns but was dressed in white. That creature stared right at me, and I woke up screaming and soaking wet. They were such diabolical creatures that from then on the insomnia got worse. As I closed my eyes and slept, I could clearly see in my dreams those infernal creatures. They would not go away. It was horrible. All of this made me helpless, confused, and frightened. I was disappointed that the ritual had made things much worse. It was the opposite of my expectation.

Moving to My Mother's House

After two days of much insomnia and fear, I went and slept at my mother's house again but this time, I slept right next to her. I needed to hold her hand. I was in a very bad state. I hadn't been in that situation since I was a little child, needing my mother to calm my fear of monsters and the dark. Only now, as an adult, I knew this was not make believe. All this made me confused and depressed because I did not understand what was happening to me. I did not tell anyone about the shamanic ritual not even my mother. At first, this was because I just didn't believe that any of it was real. I really thought that the whole ritual was just hocus pocus invented in Hollywood. But after the ritual, I was in constant, utter confusion, and fear. I could not tell anyone because my thoughts were being manipulated. My head was in a state of nothing. I could not grab a thought or do as I wanted. I lost my capability for free thinking.

One night, my mother told me to open up the Bible to Psalm 91 and to read it aloud. It was at this moment that I truly started looking for Christ for the first time in my life. On the days that followed, I would open the Bible in Spanish and start to read the New Testament for myself. I did not know what I was looking for, but I hoped to find some answers to everything that was happening to me. I was hungry for God. I wanted to find answers. I wanted meaning to my dull life. I wanted answers to all that was happening to me. I was hopeful to find these answers in the Bible. I would spend many hours reading God's Word in the many days that followed. I would read and read until bedtime. The problem was, I had sold my soul to the enemy. I was being possessed (held captive) and my soul felt great comfort when reading the Bible, especially the psalms. But since I was back with Satan, he did everything he could to end my life as soon as possible, so I could not find out the truth. When someone is looking for truth (Jesus, I am the way, the truth, and the life), Satan will do everything to get you away from it. Hence the torments.

A Little Angel

As my struggle continued, I went on a walk one night with much sadness in my heart. I was softly crying and listening to the classical music of the Iceland Symphony Orchestra. I walked slowly through the park and suddenly noticed that something was following me, actually running after me. I could not hear properly because I was listening to the music. My heart started to beat rapidly, and I thought that at any moment someone was going to hurt me. I was in such a low mood. I was depressed and fearful that this "something" was going to kill me. It was running towards me, and I started to prepare for the worst. To my surprise, it was a boy of about five years old. I looked at the child, still hearing the orchestra in my earphones. I was still in a state of fear when I turned to him. I saw his little mouth move and realized he was talking to me, so I took my headphones off and listened to him. He touched me and told me not to go that way, that the way his mum goes is a better way. I was perplexed. I did not understand why this child would touch a stranger who was dressed completely in black. You could tell by the colors that I was wearing that I was certainly not in a good mood, yet he had come running towards me in a place where there was not much light. The light posts were spaced 200 meters from each other. Furthermore, there was no light in the place that I was standing, yet he still came and touched from behind the mantle. I smiled with a teary face and told him not to worry that I was doing well. Again, I wrote to Jim about what had just happened to me, and he said that my angel had sent the boy and that everything was fine. I told him that nothing was fine, that I was very sad and with all the visions of hell I was having, I had no peace. I told him I was now living with my mother again. Basically, I told him everything. It got so bad that I was screaming at night when I had visions from hell. It was terrifying. I was in a state of panic and my mother did not know what to do except to pray. I still had not told her about the ritual. I did not tell anybody except for Jim.

The Man that Spoke Through Me

The next day, I was in the living room, when, all of a sudden, a man spoke out of my mouth. I can't remember what he was saying but my mom and I were terrified. A man speaking out of my mouth! My mother is my witness. Both of us were not thinking about demonic possession. We were busy with daily duties and talking about how to improve my sleep. Eventually we bought valerian pills and a new pillow. Unfortunately, none of it helped me, as I knew it wouldn't. I was so far removed from trying these types of fixes. Something spiritual and very dark was happening, even if I did not yet recognize what it was. If only it had been as simple as adding a new pillow and some sleeping pills but the door, I had opened would prove difficult to close.

The Little Lights in My Mother's Bathroom

A new sleeping style was being established and it provided a type of routine even if that routine was not normal. I would read the Bible to myself and then at three or four in the morning, I would fall asleep and sleep until noon. That is how the days went by and by. Until one day, I started to notice and pay attention to shiny things on the wall in my mother's bathroom. When I looked at the wall, I saw something like tiny lights. I commented again to Jim, who told me he was talking to angels, and that these tiny lights were angels that wanted to communicate with me. I thought that was strange, but interesting at the same time and since I was experiencing so many strange things, I was starting to accept that what Jim was saying could be correct. I wasn't raised in Christianity, and I did not know what I had gotten myself into. Following Jim's advice that angels were trying to communicate with me, I tried to talk to them. I would think questions like: Are you real? Are you many? Are you, my angels? These "lights" would shine brighter with a yes, and dimmer with a no. I had also read in the ritual book that when you stand still and ask a question with your mind, if the answer is yes, your body will lean forward. If the answer is no, your body will lean back. In my mind, I asked if I was going to die, and my body leaned forward. I was communicating with shiny lights. I was surprised at how these "angels" could hear my thoughts and react accordingly to them.

The Last Trip To My Apartment

After having stayed at my mother's house for some time, I decided to visit my apartment one afternoon. I took a blue IKEA bag and my big purse with me and left my mother's house. On the way, I was listening to Kanye West. I remember the details of that day so clearly. I walked to the tram stop. There I noticed that all the people around me were turning towards me and whispering. I told myself that I was imagining it. That it was all in my mind. But when I boarded the tram, the diabolic presence of oppression was an even stronger presence. I saw the faces of the people but instead of truly seeing their faces, I saw evil. They would turn towards me and laugh evilly and aloud. I realized that something was wrong, something was very wrong, but I did not understand what it was. I thought I was going mad. I could not continue to my destination on this tram because of the evil I was seeing, so I disembarked halfway there. I got out and looked at the sky, as I now clearly understood that something was not right with me, but I still could not understand what was happening. I decided to walk more than two miles to my house, hoping that the walk would take away the strange discomfort that I was feeling. I had managed to convince myself that I just needed some air.

The Car Plates #6

As I was walking, I suddenly heard a voice telling me, "Look at the license plates and follow the ones with the number six." As I looked at the license plates, I noticed that the number six shone and stood out more than the others. There were several plates with the number six on them and I followed the instruction that the voice gave to me. The instructions led me to a dead end road where a forest started. I did not fully understand what was happening. I was partly convinced that my angel was talking to me. After all, Jim had said that I had a protective angel and I had communicated with the angels in my mother's bathroom.

Later however, I would find out that 666 is the devil's mark called The Number of the Beast as described in Revelation chapter 13 in the Bible. During the whole time I was being led by the voice, I was asking God what was wrong with me. *Why is this happening to me, Lord?* I couldn't come to terms with exactly what was happening. The confusion was overwhelming.

The Forest

As I followed the voice, I reached the forest, but I did not know where to go, whether to the left or to the right. Then suddenly, I heard several voices, some said go left, others said turn right. Wrapped in so much confusion I decided to go right. Entering the woods, the voices kept whispering that I should go further in and leave the route. A thought rang out in my mind saying, "Don't leave the road or the sidewalk," so I followed the little stony path. As I walked further, my vision started to get cloudy and then my eyes stopped seeing. I was blind. I was no longer in control of my body. I now know I was under a satanic influence but at the time, I did not know. I had no idea the devil was real. I thought he was an invention of Hollywood. This influence was amazingly strong and powerful.

Supernatural Launch

There I was, in a forest completely alone full of fear and dismay with my eyes involuntarily closed, unable to understand anything. Suddenly, my spiritual eyes were opened, and I could see myself at 360 degrees around. It was as if I was outside of my body standing above myself. I saw how my arms were opened horizontally to the sides in the shape of a "t," stretched out and both hands opened simultaneously. My purse and Ikea bag hit the ground. Before I could think or see, something supernatural threw my body into the deep part of the forest. I would describe it as a wind or a power. My feet were crawling all over the wild area and my head and body were hitting all kinds of branches, leaves, and bushes. I was struck with fear but also perplexed. I was literally floating a few centimeters above the earth. I had only seen this in movies, and knew it was only created by special effects. However, I was now experiencing it for real. I have no doubt about it. But just for a few seconds I thought, "Wow! What on earth is this!?" Then I was thrown to a landing point with great force and fury, falling with my face to the ground in a fetal position. As I laid there, I heard a great voice like a roaring sound that said to me, "WHAT DID I TELL YOU?!" I had no idea where this voice was coming from. It was absolutely frightening.

I had never, not even in a theater with surround sound, heard this kind of voice. It was not human.

The False Lord's Prayer

When I heard the voice saying those words with great authority, my body began to tremble in an uncontrollable way. I was terrified to death. I found myself almost unable to breathe. I remembered that a few days prior I have investigated Occultism and the Wicca on the internet and one of its members has written an *Our Father* prayer that I had saved on my cell phone. I began to recite it. I still thought, at this time, that angels were talking to me. I had not yet realized that I was getting deeper and deeper in the demonic world. This *Our Father* prayer was a false *Our Father* prayer, but I did not know it. I was in a panic, so I grabbed my cell phone quickly and began to recite it, telling myself that this oppression would pass with the Lord's Prayer. I do not know how long I stayed in that position in the middle of that forest praying that false prayer. What I do remember is that while I was in the fetal position on the forest ground, I heard something like many motorcycles and sawing at the same time all over the forest and the sound of trees falling while I was still reciting the prayer in total fear.

Freedom from Oppression

After listening for a long time to the noise of burning saws and falling trees, suddenly my ears heard the relaxing song of the birds. As I listened to them in that green and wild environment, my fear began to slowly disappear and the trembling that shook my body ceased at once. In the end, I felt that this oppression pressing me against the earth had been removed from me. As I waited there in silence and almost without breathing, I tried to get up. I was so thankful that this oppression had left me. I felt relieved indeed.

The Announced Paralysis

My relief quickly turned to fear as I immediately realized that my legs would not move. I could only lift my head and trunk. Looking around, I no longer saw anything strange in the middle of that forest. I was completely dirty, with mud on my pants and scratches all over my face. Not feeling my lower extremities respond, I almost panicked, then once again with all my strength I leaned on a branch and only then, I managed to get up. As horrifying as this experience was, little did I know that the next day would hold an even more terrifying encounter that I call the "Imminent Happening."

Total Confusion

When I got up from the forest ground and looked around, I did not know which way to go or how to get home. I had forgotten my belongings, my bag and wallet, and in fact, I didn't remember that I had anything with me. This is what demonic possession is all about. You are not in your own mind. Your mind BELONGS to the devil, and he controls your thinking pattern when you are possessed. Luckily, I had my cell phone and the keys to my apartment in my pocket. After a long journey trying to find the exit from the forest, I finally saw a man from afar, who was leaving the forest in his vehicle. I ran up and asked him for directions. He looked at me rather surprised and informed me that I was a long way away from my village, but that I should follow the indicated path and without any problem, I would reach my destination.

Thank the Lord

As I walked along that path, I opened my arms to heaven in thanksgiving to the Lord for delivering me from such a terrible oppression. Tears began to fall from my eyes, as some passing by looked at me, and asked if they could help me in any way. I told them that everything was fine, that I was very happy, and they should not worry about me. Now looking back, of course, such behavior, walking with arms stretched out and saying aloud, THANK YOU, LORD, would alarm anybody in this unbelieving world, but at that time, I did not see it as strange. After talking to them and wishing them a nice afternoon, I continued silently on the road to my home.

At My Home

I arrived at my apartment where it was very quiet. I did not hear any voices. I sat on the floor and listened to classical music. After some time, I thought of going to my home church, a catholic basilica to get help. I understood that what had happened to me in the forest and at home, a man speaking through my mouth, was not normal. All the voices, I could not figure out what they meant or why I would hear them. Why would they talk to me? I realized that all these voices I heard and the evil faces on the tram were something supernatural, which in my understanding meant that I needed help from a priest or monk. I was hoping and praying that a trip to the basilica would provide me the opportunity to receive the help I needed.

The Trip to the Basilica

On my way to the basilica, I reflected over and over again on the voices, the oppression in the woods, and the luminous license plates, and it all seemed oddly strange to me. The basilica was a place I used to visit almost every Sunday as a Catholic. In the months prior to the ritual, I felt the urge to visit the basilica more frequently. Getting there was complicated because the buses would drive the sharp route only once every hour. It was also a good way into winter already and I felt the cold biting into my skin.

The Bus

I waited for the bus, but it did not come. I asked some people who owned vehicles if they could give me a lift. For some reason, they all refused. I told myself that something strange was going on because no buses were arriving, and no one wanted to give me a lift. Then after waiting for almost an hour, one bus came.

When the bus arrived, I felt a bit happier because soon I would be talking to one of the monks or priests who would surely help me. I was determined. I remember, as the bus drove, I could see in the distance a very large full moon. It was so big that I felt intimidated by it.

At the Basilica

On arrival at the basilica, it was very dark. I only saw an older woman with her mother in the parking lot. I went up to her to ask her something like if she believed that this religion, "The Catholic" religion was the true one. She answered without me saying a word, "Don't worry darling, here you are in the good one!" I was very scared and surprised. How could she possibly read my mind? Then she rang at the monks' door and one of them came down dressed completely in black and said, "They are waiting for her!" Once again, I was absolutely confused. Why would they know that I was going to ask for help? How could this possibly be? I was very perplexed. Even though I was experiencing confusion, I decided to go and get help anyway because this was a very familiar place for me. It used to be my church.

Manipulation of Lights

I approached the monk's house where they were supposedly waiting for me. Now the lights in the building went on when I approached it and went off when I made two steps back. I could not see anybody in the building. But I tested what I was seeing with the lights five times! Step forward, lights on, step back, lights off, step forward, lights on, step back, lights off. I couldn't believe what I was seeing with my own eyes. I was worried and with the confusion I already had from the woman and the monk, I didn't know what to do. I was so desperate to be free from this oppression and the unexplainable things that were happening to me. I took up all my courage and rang the bell to see if one of the monks would come down to meet me, but nobody came. I rang repeatedly. After some time, a monk came. He wanted to know what I wanted and told me he didn't have time for me now, as they were about to have dinner.

Jesus

I was disappointed with his answer, but while we were standing in the entrance, I saw a bronze statue of Jesus and Mary behind him, and I told the monk that I knew Him. I just could not say Jesus' name. Pointing at the statue of Jesus the monk said to me, "That's Jesus, the Lord." I was on the border of a breakdown. I saw this monk and thought, "He will help me" and then it just came out of my mouth. I told the monk that it was possible that I was possessed as I was not feeling very well and had been having supernatural experiences. I told him that so many strange things had happened to me that day and I was completely alone and didn't understand what was going on! I begged him to help and pray for me. He put a hand on my head and said a prayer. He said that exorcism was very dangerous, and that people have died from it. He said the indicated person who performed exorcisms was far away and it was not so easy to contact him. I thanked him for everything.

I left even more confused, and still in fear. I thought of calling my mother and telling her that everything was okay, but my cell phone's battery was almost dead. I decided to go to a restaurant that was nearby, to borrow a charger for my cell phone. When I went inside, I asked a waiter if I could borrow one and he immediately answered that he would bring me one, but soon after that, he said he was sorry that he could not lend it to me anymore. Again, surprised but disappointed, I left that place. I left thinking how strange it was that he first wanted to lend me the charger and then he changed his mind so quickly. My confusion started to become a giant in my mind. It was making me question everything and everyone. I desperately wanted to know what was going on with me and how to make it stop.

> *1 Corinthians 14:33*
> *For God is not the author of confusion*
> *but of peace (…)*

The Man and the Dog

I started on the road towards home when I saw a young man with a tiny dog. I went up to him and asked him immediately if I could borrow his cellphone just to call my mother and let her know that everything was okay. He agreed and handed me his cellphone. My mother took the call and her voice sounded desperate and very worried, so I told her that I was fine, but I could not tell her where I was. The voices made me fearful of telling my mom and prevented me from doing so. I knew something was controlling my mind because I could not think clearly anymore. I was fearful of the entity that was dominating me. I hung up and returned the cellphone. I asked this man in his mid-thirties if he could take me to the station, because of the location the buses wouldn't drive anymore. He said yes. I got into his vehicle.

While driving the young man suddenly began to behave in a very rough way. He began to yell at me like a madman telling me, *"I will bring you now to the place where the accident happened!"* I answered him, "No! I don't want you to bring me anywhere other than the tram stop. Please!" He then rushed like a madman with his tiny dog barking non-stop. I was terrified and was just waiting for the car to stop. When we reached the tram station, he quickly drove out and yelled at me, "LEAVE!" And I immediately left that madman and his car. I was so relieved that I had escaped this trap.

Arriving home. I locked myself in and suddenly I felt the oppression again. My head became foggy, and I couldn't see clearly. I walked around all throughout the apartment with my head down. I lay down on the floor and I started listening to Chopin and formed my body into a "T" shape. I was not myself anymore. I heard the voices telling me that *I was going to die*. The voices got louder and louder. At 3 o'clock in the morning, I decided to call my Christian uncle and my grandmother from the Dominican Republic and ask them if it was true that I had to die. My grandmother replied that whoever told me that was a great liar. That I did not have to listen to those voices. She also said that my uncle was in his room praying, regretting that he could not be with me at that point in time. She said, "He is surely praying for you." I was a bit sad but said it was okay.

The Call to My Mother

While talking to my grandmother, she asked me about my mother, and I told her that I hadn't heard from her really. My grandmother insisted that I call my mother. When I finished the call with my grandmother, I decided to call my mother even though it was later than 3:00 in the morning. My mother answered the call in a state of nail biting worry and panic telling me to stay exactly where I was. I learned that she was in a panic because the blue IKEA bag and handbag I had left in the woods has been found by somebody who brought it to the police station. The police contacted my mother telling her that they had my bag, and she should come down to collect it. She said, "Your father and I will come to pick you up right now." I could hear the anxiety in her voice and knew that she was worried sick about me. My parents then came at around 4am to pick me up and we went to my mother's place. I remember them both telling me, "From tomorrow onwards everything will get better."

December 15, 2016

Once in my mother's apartment, we both lay in her bed. She said a prayer and I fell asleep. At about seven in the morning, I woke up. My mother scolded me and told me to go back to sleep because I hadn't slept enough, and it was still too early. However, I didn't listen to her. I shut her mouth with my hands and signaled her to be quiet by putting my index finger to my lips. Then I put my hands over her ears. This was utterly strange for me to do. I would never do this to my mother. Nothing made any sense at all. I seemed to remain in a complete state of utter confusion. I got up, went silently to the bathroom, and locked myself in.

Demonic cries

In the bathroom, I laid down on the floor. I remember the window of the bathroom being wide open. After some minutes of being silent on the bathroom floor, I started to scream extremely loud. I went through seven different scream levels. The screams ranged from very deep male voices to very high female voices. I screamed seven different times. My whole body shook, and my head was banging against the stone floor. I think I was in this state for about 15 minutes. When I finished screaming, I stood up and looked at myself in the mirror. All I could see in the mirror was me. I expected to look different or somehow not be myself, but I couldn't see anything strange or weird. I remember thinking, "Now I am free of whatever was in me!" However, I assume the opposite was the case.

I had been possessed. Once again, I heard a voice and it said to me, "Now, you are a six-year-old girl." During the screams, my mother had gone quickly to pick up my father. She was a bundle of nerves, and when they arrived, they didn't know what to expect. The screaming had finished thankfully, but my mother was quite traumatized about all the frightening events that had just occurred to me.

I acted and greeted my parents like a six-year-old girl. My parents were shocked to see me act this way. I could see everything, but I could not do anything about it. It was as if I was locked in my own body. I very tenderly sat on my father's lap. A voice told me that he had hurt me so badly (a lie) that he had to die, and that I would have to kill him. My father had been very concerned about my behavior. He is a very intelligent person and has always been my best advisor because of his great intellect. He was a tender loving father and would never hurt me, so I shouted at this voice saying, "No! I cannot kill my father and I cannot kill my mother!" Then I began to be very afraid and terrified as the voices told me that my parents were the ones who would kill me if I did not kill them.

The Persecution

I began to believe with all my heart what all those voices that were speaking to me. They terrified the life out of me, so much so, that I dressed quickly and ran away from home. That is when the chase started. My dad was in the car behind me, and my mother was running after me on foot. My mother was screaming,

"Malena, Malena wait!" I was running and jumping like a six-year-old girl and stopping vehicles in the street, because the voices were telling me that I had supernatural powers. I remember that my mother followed me to the building that I entered, and after giving her a hug I pushed her out of the doorway with great strength. This was very strange because I found that I was in the building where the lawyer that I had hired to fight my case for unemployment had an office. I had been there once, but only to put some documents in the mailbox. I had never seen her face to face, and I did not understand why I was there. I proceeded walking up to the fifth floor. The secretary let me in. I asked for the lawyer and she told me that she was at court. Then I calmly took a seat in the waiting area. Immediately, the secretary got a call and while she was attending to that call, I left and locked myself in an office where I sat down in a chair in front of a computer. The desktop showed a picture of a man with a big yellow plastic tube in a pool. As I looked at that picture, two red horns grew out of that man's head in such a gigantic way. I was terrified. Suddenly, my eyes were closed again. I saw everything in red until I could not see a thing again. I was blind.

My Last Prayer to the Lord

I got out of that chair in front of the computer, knelt down, and prayed to the Lord that if my time had come, He should take me with Him. While praying, I heard a knock on the door from outside with great force. It was the secretary shouting, telling me to open it. While I was still on my knees, this powerful force came over me, like the one in the forest, and it threw me against the windows.

Satan

My eyes would not open. It was as if they were blindfolded by some external power. I felt my body floating and while in that suspended state, great silence and stillness followed. I felt a blow to my head but there was nothing there and all I could see was the color red. I found myself on the 5th floor of this building, on the outside of the windows but I was not really standing on the windowsill, I was floating above it. It was then that I saw a stunning light and heard a beautiful voice say to me, "*DAUGHTER, COME WHERE I AM. YOU WON'T SUFFER ANYMORE.*" I could feel a force pushing me from outside the windows backwards into the office, but I said, "No, let me go, I want to go to my Lord Jesus. I want to be with Christ!"

The Fall

After saying that I want to be with the Lord, I fell five stories down. I wanted to embrace the Lord or go to Him by walking up to Him. I was floating all that time, maybe two minutes at least and I really thought I could just walk to the Lord and He would rescue me. I thought it was Him talking to me. As I fell, I never felt my heart fail, or my mind lose consciousness. I heard an evil cry from my mouth while I was falling down, and then right away I heard the little birds singing. I felt as if I was being held.

Thanks to the Lord, a woman who was in the bank office near the building heard the evil cry and looked just then outside the window. She ran frantically to the backyard, dropped her coffee and keys to the ground, and screamed on the street that a girl had fallen from a window. My mother followed her and other people to the backyard where they found me laying there on the ground. A few minutes later, the ambulance arrived, and I was taken to the hospital. I was calm the whole time but as soon as I heard my mother cry I was fainting and coming back.

Though I do not remember all the details of that day, I later found out that I, or rather the demon talking through me, said to the police officer, "Leave me all alone! Satan is coming for me very soon!" This was read from the police report when the lawyer fighting my disability case with the insurance company re-stated in her plea that it was not a suicide attempt. I did not try to kill myself that day. I was possessed by demons who tried to kill me.

Seven Creatures

I woke up in the shock room in the hospital, a room where you are scanned from head to toe. I heard a big noise and woke up. Looking around me, I realized that I was in an x-ray room. I saw that seven black creatures had gathered together on top of me. Today I know these were demons. They were staring at me and screaming at me, "Maria! Maria! Die! Die!" This name stemmed from a time after I had done the ritual. I was at my mother's house, and I heard a voice tell me that

I am like Maria from the Bible. As I was Catholic at the time, I thought of Maria (Mary), the mother of Jesus and I replied that it was impossible that I was like her. How could that be? In hindsight, I was more like Maria of Magdalene who had seven demons. I was perplexed and replied to them, "My name is Malena. What do you want from me?" They kept shouting at me, "Maria, Die! Die!" one by one and coming very close to my face. In their faces, I could only see the naked hatred and contempt for humanity. Then I fainted and woke up after sixteen hours of surgery later.

The fall had shattered my feet and damaged my spine and spinal cord yet none of my organs were damaged. Even though I am now a full-time wheelchair user, I know the Lord decided to extend His mercy to me that day, as He did not let me die. The fact is, had I died that day I would be in Hell, for I had not yet put Christ on through baptism. God's Word teaches us in Galatians 3:27, "For as many of you as were baptized into Christ have put on Christ." I thank the Lord immensely that He spared my life from eternal death on the day of The Imminent Happening.

Amen.

Chapter 2:
Demon Possession

Much of what I have talked about regarding demonic oppression is how it can come with the occult and by participating in occultic practices, whether knowingly or unknowingly. However, as was the case with me, oppression can lead to demon possession.

In many cultures today, demon possession is not talked about or acknowledged. Again, Satan has caused it to be a taboo topic that is often swept under the rug even within churches. However, if we look at the New Testament, we see that casting out demons from demon possessed people was a common, regular practice of both Jesus and the disciples.

In many cultures, we call demon possession by other names. We call it bad behavior, genetics, or psychopathic. We sometimes even call it mental illness. This is not to say that all mental illness is demonic. It is just to state that when it is demonic, it gets labeled as something else entirely. We try to treat it with medication, therapy, counseling, and behavior modification. This is another deception of Satan. He has caused the hearts and minds of unbelievers to be so blinded that they do not acknowledge God or Satan. To say that evil is inside of someone through demon possession is to acknowledge the existence of demons and Satan, to acknowledge the existence of demons is to acknowledge the existence of angels and God. We live in a time of grand ignorance. We see evil taking place. We see evil increasing. We see individuals perpetrating great atrocities, yet we do want to acknowledge that a person can be possessed and controlled by demons who are bent on doing evil. We see evil all the time, but seldom do we acknowledge that the evil comes from demon possession.

There are many cultures, however, where witchcraft is taught, participated in, and accepted as a cultural norm. The demon possession that can take place, due to this, is thought to be because the person who went to the witch doctor or participated in a spell or ritual, did something wrong or is evil or did not follow the commands presented. The responsibility of the demon possession is placed on the person's character not on their willingness to participate. For example, in South Africa, the Zulu accept both the Inyanga and the Isangoma. The Isangoma are witch doctors who are considered religious leaders and often use trances are a means to communicate with the dead. The Inyanga are witchdoctors who are "healers" (Diskin, Eben. "9 Countries Where Witchcraft Is Still Practiced - or Persecuted." Matador Network, September 9, 2020. https://matadornetwork.com/read/countries-witchcraft-exists-practiced/). They claim to have powers to heal those who are sick or afflicted. According to the Christian church in South Africa, these practices have led to an increase in demon possession. However, instead of acknowledging that these practices lead to demonic possession, it is believed that the power and rituals of the witchdoctors reveal a demon or evil that is already within the person, so the cycle continues.

In Mexico, witchcraft is practiced through the belief in and worship of Santa Muerte, the Saint of Death. Statues of her are said to hold dark magical powers that can be channeled by those who want to use dark magic. This practice has increased greatly, and the Catholic Church in Mexico believes that the rise in crime and drug cartels is a direct result of demonic possession through the revering and honoring of Saint Muerte. It has gone so far that priests are having to ask for help with exorcisms. According to an article by the BBC, "It is estimated that the cult, whose followers worship a skull in a wedding dress carrying a scythe, has some eight million followers in Mexico - and more among Mexican migrants in Central America, the US and Canada" (Hernandez, Vladimir. "The Country Where Exorcisms Are on the Rise." BBC News. BBC, November 26, 2013. https://www.bbc.com/news/magazine-25032305.).

Stories and practices such as these can also be seen in Venezuela, Chile, Haiti, Romania, Saudi Arabia, and the Philippines and in so many more countries around the world. It is clear that where there is witchcraft, there is demon possession.

This does not mean that everyone is vulnerable to demonic possession. Satan and demons cannot possess human life, without the human first giving him permission to do so (when practicing occultism, witchcraft etc.). Most times, the evil spirt will enter a person and lay claim to their life due to satanic practices. As mentioned before, this could be through a séance, Ouija board, a ritual, and other practices within the occult. There are times where demons can enter through sinful lifestyle choices such as drug use or sexual deviancy opening the door to the demonic.

Demonic possession is very real, as I have testified to. My obedience to the instructions provided in the shamanic ritual and my willingness to participate in what had been sanctioned by Satan, led me to become demon possessed. Demon possession is not always black and white. There are different severities of possession, but it is important to acknowledge that when we open the door to the demonic and the occult, we are opening ourselves up to possession.

Chapter 3:
The Devil is a Real Persona

We have an adversary. He is called Satan or the Devil or Lucifer.

Satan: the chief evil spirit; the great adversary of humanity

The Devil: the chief evil spirit; Satan

Lucifer: a proud, rebellious archangel, identified as Satan, who fell from heaven, meaning "light bringer"

    He is the Father of all Lies. In John 8:44 Jesus tells us about Satan and how he operates. "You are of *your* father the devil, and the desires of your father you want to do. He was a murderer from the beginning, and does not stand in the truth, because there is no truth in him. When he speaks a lie, he speaks from his own *resources,* for he is a liar and the father of it."

    During my time in the hospital and rehabilitation center, I had a lot of time to rewind and replay all the events leading up to my fall from the window. It took me a considerable amount of time to realize and accept what had actually happened to me. I wrote to my friends, including Jim, in March 2017, informing them that I was in the hospital paralyzed. I couldn't write the reason because I was still figuring out what had happened to me. I wasn't able to trace back, at that stage, all the pieces of my odyssey. There were pieces of that puzzle floating in my mind looking for their correct places. My odyssey had spaces and gaps that I was unable to fill at that time.

While reading the Bible, I began to understand that the Devil is a real persona. He is an evil spirit that is only around to steal, kill, and destroy (John 10:10) and unfortunately, I had made a covenant with the Devil when I agreed to proceed with that shamanic ritual. Many people dismiss the Devil and relabel demonic, satanic activity. It is now disguised in new, seemingly harmless terms like New Age, Astrology, and "Fantasy" movies that celebrate witchcraft. I am distressed that many people, especially young people, are so smitten with this New Age Movement. They are being absorbed by all the shining lights and lies of New Age. Do not be fooled, our adversary, the devil, is not stupid. He knows how to present his diabolical tactics in white, energized, light. 2nd Corinthians 11:14 tells us, "And no wonder! For Satan himself transforms himself into an angel of light." It is with great dismay that I see how easily people, both young and old, are pulled into witchcraft. Not really believing that Satan exists, helps him and his demons, immensely.

Had I talked to a Christian person before committing such an atrocity, I would never have done it.

I neither told my mother about my plans nor did I speak to my family about it. I acted totally on my own authority. This happens many times. The lion will isolate and single out its prey. Away from the security and protection of the rest of the herd, it is vulnerable. The lion will attack and devour. Satan is referred to as a "lion" in 1 Peter 5:8 which says, "Be sober, be vigilant; because your adversary the devil walks about like a **roaring lion**, seeking whom he may devour."

He and his demons or helpers are exactly the same. Divide and conquer is their trademark. When their victims are isolated and alone, then evil wins. All I can say to parents and young adults is to watch out. Be very careful with witchcraft and do not practice it in any form whatsoever. It is highly dangerous, and its ending can be deadly. It is difficult to find any reliable source on the internet about cases of people being demon possessed because demon possession is dismissed as so many other things.

Some demon possessed people experience an untimely death. As was the case with Anneliese Michel. I don't know what she did, that got herself into a demon possessed state. Apparently, she came from a Catholic family. Catholics pray to images and idols, and many do not know that doing so is an abomination to the Lord (Deuteronomy 7:25) (Exodus 20:4-6). They are often taught that they are actually using these items to draw closer to God. A lack of understanding of idol worship, the New Age, and witchcraft does not prevent someone from falling into its clutches.

Unknowingly, I had made a covenant with the devil when I did that shamanic ritual and as a result,

I became demon possessed. When Judas betrayed our Lord Jesus Christ for 30 silver pieces in Matthew 27:3-5, Satan entered into him (John 13:27). He had sold his soul to the devil for thirty pieces of silver. I had sold my soul for the chance of sleeping again. Many people do not know that they are making a covenant with the Devil when practicing New Age or when they practice these rituals. You lose control over yourself, as you perceive that there is a strange power chasing after you. You are not yourself anymore as you are being manipulated in a supernatural way. As long as you don't object, everything is fine. **But if you were like me, looking for Christ, the way, the truth, and the life (John 14:6) then you are getting into some serious trouble.** This is because before you are a Christian, you are of the Devil.1 John 5:19 says, "We know that we are of God, and the whole world lies under the sway of the wicked one." Ephesians 2:2 tells us, "In which you once walked according to the course of this world, according to the prince of the power of the air, the spirit who now works in the sons of disobedience." As long as you are not a Christian, he will not harm you really, because you are already his. It is only through Jesus Christ, when you put on Jesus Christ in baptism that you become a child of God (Acts 2:38). When a human being starts to look and search for the truth in Christ, a spiritual war is starting regarding your soul. You have started a titanic spiritual war and it is about your soul's final destination, heaven or hell for your soul and this will be for eternity. The devil will try to steal, kill, and destroy your faith. Ephesians 6:10-13 says, "Finally, my brethren, be strong in the

Lord and in the power of His might. Put on the whole armor of God, that you may be able to stand against the wiles of the devil. For we do not wrestle against flesh and blood, but against principalities, against powers, against the rulers of the darkness of this age, against spiritual hosts of wickedness in the heavenly places. Therefore, take up the whole armor of God, that you may be able to withstand in the evil day, and having done all, to stand."

The messengers of Satan often come across as being so full of light and peace, unless they are members of satanic cults but even then, they can disguise themselves. This is how it was with my friend Jim. He did not seem at all evil. A bit different from the rest of the world, you could say a lost soul with a longing for spiritual things, which is why he was into everything. A little bit of Buddhism, a little bit of shamans, and a little bit of Yoga. New Age offers so many choices. It is everywhere. Be it Yoga, be it Transcendental Meditation or Ayahuasca. It all sounds so attractive. Refreshing even. You will go beyond yourself. Get in touch with the inner you. You can heal yourself. You. You. You. You are your own little god. You would never think that behind all of that is the Devil and his demons. Satan and his evil forces understand human beings better than we understand ourselves. They have been around since the beginning. How is it that you get into the claws of the Devil and his demons? It is always a necessity, an urge towards self: self-governance, self-reliance, self-promotion, and self-worship.

We see this in the Garden of Eden. Eve was looking at the forbidden fruit with lust of her eyes, the lust of her flesh, and the pride of life. Eve was allured to the fruit on the tree of good and evil by the eye-gate. Her eyes looked at it as being good, and it appealed to her desire to fulfill herself. Her first mistake was to enter into a dialogue with Satan. She listened to what he had to say. It made sense to her, and his seemly good reasons were easy to understand and follow. She bought Satan's lie wholeheartedly. Her first step into her fall was to look and keep looking at that which God had forbidden (Genesis 3:1-7). So, we keep looking at the things that seem so harmless to us, but good for the eye, and we buy the lie, and it can have disastrous results on our lives like it had in mine. I didn't die, thanks to the Lord Jesus Christ, but I am now paralyzed from the waist down. I will live with these consequences for the rest of my life unless the Lord restores me. Even though these are my circumstances, I do not give up my hope.

Another story in the Bible that shows how the Devil works with humans is the story of Saul from Tarsus. He used to chase down the early Christians. He would stop at nothing, just to hunt down the believers in Jesus Christ. He murdered and locked up many Christians. Here we can clearly see how the Devil used Saul for his purposes. The Devil is against everything that is holy, true, and Christ-centered. He is after the soul of man. He hates Jesus and His children and wants to kill them, steal from them, and destroy them. He will use, through his lies, whoever and whatsoever to accomplish this (John 8:44). But, thanks to the great mercies of our Lord Jesus Christ, He encountered Saul on his way to go after Christians in Damascus and asked him, "Saul, Saul, why are you persecuting Me? I am Jesus, whom you are persecuting," (Acts 9:4-5). Saul had a conversion experience and the Lord used Saul, who was later called the Apostle Paul, greatly in the ministry of the conversion of the Jews first and later the Gentiles. He turned his hatred, which he had out of ignorance, into love for the Christians and he got baptized too. That is how he became a Christian and we today can become Christians just like that.

Like Saul, I was on the wrong side of the game and the Lord Jesus Christ had abundant mercy on me when he saved me from death. At my death, my soul would have landed down in torment. Because I was not baptized for the remissions of my sins and without the forgiveness of the remission of sins by washing them away in baptism, which is a burial in water, you cannot enter the kingdom of God. John 3:5-8 says, "Jesus answered, "Most assuredly, I say to you, unless one is born of water and the Spirit, he cannot enter the kingdom of God. That which is born of the flesh is flesh, and that which is born of the Spirit is spirit. Do not marvel that I said to you, 'You must be born again.' The wind blows where it wishes, and you hear the sound of it, but cannot tell where it comes from and where it goes. So is everyone who is born of the Spirit."

Not in a million years would I have thought that this seemingly harmless shamanic ritual would cause me to become demon possessed and paralyzed changing my life forever. It all seemed harmless since I didn't believe in evil spirits or the Devil. I really thought they were just an invention of Hollywood and if it didn't work, then I would find another solution, maybe by moving out. I looked desperately for peace to sleep but all I found was tragedy. A human tragedy conducted by the devil and his demons through a shamanic ritual. Not believing that the devil exists does not exclude us from his tactics and control. But through this tragedy, I found the One who forgives any sin and wants me to be forever in Heaven. We have to decide while we are on earth, where we want to live in eternity. It is either in hell, which was created for the devil and his demons, where according to Mark 9:48, "Their worm does not die, and the fire is not quenched." Or in Heaven where according to Revelation 21:21-22, "The twelve gates were twelve pearls: each individual gate was of one pearl. And the street of the city was pure gold, like transparent glass. But I saw no temple in it, for the Lord God Almighty and the Lamb are its temple."

You ought to choose wise and well!

Chapter 4:
My Conversion Story

When I first woke up in the hospital, I did not understand where I was or why I was in the emergency room. I asked a nurse and she looked at me and said, "I hope you regret what you did." In her mind, she was thinking I had tried to commit suicide. I asked her, "What? Why? What did I do?" She went on her way leaving me in a state of confusion because I did not remember what happened.

A young psychiatrist came into emergency ward and started asking me questions. He wanted to know why I had done what I had done. He wanted to know what my motives were. I could not answer these questions because I was still confused and unclear about what had taken place. At this point, everyone, including my parents, thought that I had attempted suicide. I told the psychiatrist that I did not attempt suicide. I did not even remember what I had done. I was eventually told that I jumped out of a window around fifteen meters high. I told him that all of this must be a misunderstanding. I didn't know why I was in the hospital. I could NOT remember anything. It was like there was a hole in my memory. Only after several months did my memory come back piece-by-piece. I remember that I feared turning on my cellphone and seeing what messages I may have sent before my accident. My accident happened on December 15th and I did not activate my cellphone until end of March. When I opened my messages, I had nicely written to Jim and to some other acquaintances, but I did not find any goodbye-message or anything else to suggest suicide.

    I was adamant with the psychiatrist that I did not attempt suicide. He diagnosed me with temporary schizophrenic psychosis. Seemingly, I finally had a reason for what I had been through (or so I thought) and back then I fully believed the diagnosis. I did not understand why I did what I did. I had no clue what happened to me. I was thinking and overthinking, and nothing made sense to me so his diagnosis was something I could try to make sense of. I even informed my friends in March that it seems I had a temporary schizophrenic psychosis. I now know that this was not the case. I do not believe I am a person with schizophrenia. I never had an episode before my fall. In order to be diagnosed with schizophrenia, you need to have several episodes and I did not have that. I was demon possessed and this possession led to me having no control over my mind, body, or actions. The average person does not believe that demon possession is real, just as I did not believe it was real until it happened to me. Think about it. Can a person with schizophrenia change their voice suddenly from female to male, just like that? I don't think so.

From the beginning, they gave me anti-depressants because they assumed my diagnosis of paraplegia (paralysis) would make me depressed. As time went by and I still could not move my legs, I received the confirmation from my traumatologist and the plastic surgeons that I might not walk ever again. I became very sad. Then the traumatologist told me that I had bacteria in my feet, and they would need to cut open my feet and cut out all the infected tissue and bone. I told him, "Cut my legs off!" I had resigned any hope. I could not get a hold of what had happened to me. First the doctors were saying I was mentally ill (temporary schizophrenia) and then they said I would never walk again. Add to that the news that they needed to cut open my feet every Monday, Wednesday, and Friday for at least one month and that, it did not look good. I was heartbroken, devastated, and absolutely confused.

While I was coming to grips with everything that had happened and was happening to me, I continued to see terrible things when I tried to sleep and visions when I was awake. I saw monsters and all kind of very strange things. I remember vividly, when I had closed my eyes, that I was in some kind of dark vineyard. Something very dangerous and evil was chained there. A dog? I was running in that dark vineyard and this evil monster thing was chasing me back and forth. I was awake when I had this "vision." I remember that I crawled under the bed sheets and was sweating terribly. There was no doubt about it, Satan was still in control.

During my long stay at the hospital, I was initially visited by a Catholic woman who worked at the hospital as a pastoral counselor, as I was a Catholic back then. She visited me almost every day and told me about the Lord. I remember my mother brought me a silver rosary and I would hold the cross in my hands, talk, and cry out to God. I did not understand why I was paralyzed from the waist down. At the same time, a man named Fred from the church staff of the protestant church, who worked at the hospital as well, came to visit me. I was crying as he entered the room. He started to say godly things, encourage me, and tell me citations from the Bible about fear, because I told him I was in fear. I told him I saw all kind of strange things when I tried to relax and sleep. He would ask me what kind of worship (inside the hospital) I wanted to participate in on Sundays. I told him the Catholic way of worship. Fred eventually gave me a New Testament Bible. He would come to visit and show me encouraging verses to uplift me. In the beginning, I was afraid to read the Bible because I assumed that it would touch me deeply. I was very fragile at that time, crying every day. I was very sad. Fred would come up almost daily to see how I was and cheer me up. I was also going to Catholic mass every Sunday in my bed (with many other patients), and it lifted my spirit. For the next six months, I was searching the Scriptures alone to understand and to look for the reason why all of this had happened to me.

When I was ready, I told Fred what I remembered what had happened to me. By then it must have been the end of July and the puzzle pieces were beginning to come together. I was starting to remember. I told him that I remembered that a man spoke through my mouth, and that I cried different types of cries from very high to very low on the bathroom floor at my mother's house. I told him I did a shamanic ritual to cleanse my apartment and that from then on, I was persecuted. I told him I was haunted with nightmares and visions. I told him piece by piece what I would remember, and he told me to write everything down, which I did. He gave me Bible verses about the Devil and demons that showed me this was a real battle. He told me I had a great testimony that I needed to share with the world. God had chosen me to live and not die, so I could talk about all the dangers of New Age because it is purely diabolical. Fred was one of the few people that was around after this tragedy. Almost everybody vanished except for him. He would also come to the rehabilitation center where I was staying for the next five months. There I painfully learnt everything from getting up alone, to dressing, showering, and bowel management.

I remember that Fred pointed out the book of Job to me. I found it terrible that the enemy received God's permission to touch Job and his whole family. It was too much for me at that time to read. Then he revealed to me that when you read to the end of the book of Job, you see that God gave him back everything doubled. That is where my desire to know the living God who saved me from death on that beautiful winter day of December 15, 2016, began.

I began again to read the Gospels. I started with John and fell in love with the Lord Jesus Christ more and more. I still did not understand why the Lord allowed everything that had happened to me to take place, but He is Sovereign. I learned that all things work together for good for those who love the Lord and are called according to His purpose (Romans 8:28).

As I was reading the Gospels and talking every day to my now uncle in Christ, Uncle José, overseas, he told me that it was time to look for a Church of Christ to baptize me. The Church of Christ is the church of the New Testament in the Bible. In the Bible, it speaks only of one body (church), one faith, and one baptism (Ephesians 1:22/23, Ephesians 4:4, Ephesians 5:23). It is based on the doctrine of Christ and the Apostles. I contacted the Church of Christ in my city and the preacher came to give me classes while I was back in the hospital due to my bacteria in the feet. After many conversations and reading and studying together, I decided that on the first day I was to be discharged from the hospital (September 8, 2017), I would be baptized for the forgiveness of my sins and be added to the Church of Christ by the Lord.

The steps of salvation are the following:
1) **Hear the Gospel** (Gospel = Jesus died for our sins, He was buried, and He was raised on the third day) Romans 10:17
2) **Believe in Jesus** John 3:16
3) **Repent** (change your mindset/turn away from sin) Luke 13:3
4) **Confess Jesus** Romans 10:9,
5) **Be baptized** for the remissions of your sins (by immersion) Acts 2:36-47/22:16
6) **Be faithful** Revelation 2:10/Philippians 2:12

Why was I baptized? Because I understood throughout my stay in the hospital that I was far from the grace of God. I read it in the Bible (Romans 3:23). Although grace reached out to me, during the demon possession, liberation, and the fall from fifteen meters, I understood that I was still under the evil one (1 John 5:19). But Christ came to undo the works of the Devil and give us life and life in abundance (John 10:10). Christ bore all my terrible sins one by one on the Cross of Calvary. All those who want to be saved and believe in Jesus Christ as their Lord and Savior obey the command of the Lord Jesus Christ to be baptized by immersing themselves into water: to die to self and sin and be resurrected with Christ through baptism. I did that on September 8, 2017, just nine months after my imminent accident where the Devil and his fallen angels, the demons, deceived me and I fell fifteen meters to the ground. I am now a daughter of the living and most high God. I belong to His church, which is His body, the church of Christ.

Chapter 5:

The Lord's church, the Church of Christ

The information in this chapter is from Joe R. Barnett, a church of Christ member, and is used with permission.

You have probably heard of churches of Christ and perhaps you've asked, "Who are these people? What—if anything—distinguishes them from the thousands of other churches in the world?" You may have wondered: What is their historical background? How many members do they have? What is their message? How are they governed? How do they worship? What do they believe about the Bible? I would like to take the time to answer some of these questions.

How Many Members?

Worldwide there are some 20,000 congregations of churches of Christ with a total of two and a half to three million individual members. There are small congregations, consisting of just a few members – and large ones made up of several thousand members.

The greatest concentration of numerical strength in churches of Christ is in the southern United States of America where, for instance, there are about 40,000 members in some 135 congregations in Nashville, Tennessee. In Dallas, Texas, where there are approximately 36,000 members in sixty-nine congregations. In such states as Tennessee, Texas, Oklahoma, Alabama, Kentucky – and others – there is a church of Christ in practically every town, no matter how large or small.

While the number of congregations and members is not so numerous in other places, there are churches of Christ in every state in the United States and in 109 other countries.

People of Restoration Spirit

Members of churches of Christ are a people of restoration spirit – wanting to restore in our time the original New Testament church.

Dr. Hans Kung, a well-known European theologian, published a book a few years ago entitled "The Church" (Küng, Hans. *The Church*. London: Burns & Oates, 1995.). Dr. Kung lamented the fact that the established church has lost its way, has become burdened down with tradition, and has failed to be what Christ planned it should be. The only answer, according to Dr. Kung, is to go back to the scriptures to see what the church was in its beginning, and then to recover in the twentieth century the essence of the original church. This is what churches of Christ are seeking to do.

In the latter part of the 18th century, men of different denominations, studying independently of each other, in various parts of the world, began to ask: Why not go back beyond denominationalism to the simplicity and purity of the first-century church? Why not take the Bible alone and once again continue "steadfastly in the apostles' teaching..." (Acts 2:42)? Why not plant the same seed (the Word of God, Luke 8:11) that first century Christians planted, and be Christians only, as they were? They were pleading with everyone to throw off denominationalism, to throw away human creeds, and to follow only the Bible. They taught that nothing should be required of people as acts of faith except that which is evident in the scriptures. They emphasized that going back to the Bible does not mean the establishment of another denomination, but rather a return to the original church.

Members of churches of Christ are enthusiastic about this approach. With the Bible as our only guide, we seek to find what the original church was like and restore it exactly. We do not see this as arrogance, but the very opposite. We are saving that we do not have the right to ask for men's allegiance to a human organization-but only the right to call upon men to follow God's blueprint. Not A Denomination.

For this reason, we are not interested in man-made creeds, but simply in the New Testament pattern. We do not conceive of ourselves as being a denomination – as Catholic, Protestant, or Jewish – but simply as members of the church, which Jesus established and for which He died. And that, incidentally, is why we wear His name. The term "church of Christ" is not used as a denominational designation, but rather as a descriptive term indicating that the church belongs to Christ. We recognize our own personal shortcomings and weaknesses – and this is all the more reason for wanting to carefully follow the all-sufficient and perfect plan God has for the church.

Unity Based Upon The Bible

Since God has vested "all authority" in Christ (Matthew 28:18), and since he serves as God's spokesman today (Hebrews 1:1,2), it is our conviction that only Christ has the authority to say what the church is and what we should teach. Since only the New Testament sets forth Christ's instructions to his disciples, it alone must serve as the basis for all religious teaching and practice. This is fundamental with members of churches of Christ. We believe that teaching the New Testament without modification is the only way to lead men and women to become Christians.

We believe religious division is bad. Jesus prayed for unity (John 17). And later, the apostle Paul begged those who were divided to unite in Christ (1 Corinthians 1). We believe the only way to achieve unity is by a return to the Bible. Compromise cannot bring unity. And surely no person, or group of people, has the right to draw up a set of rules by which everyone must abide. But it is altogether proper to say, "Let's unite by just following the Bible." This is fair. This is safe. This is right.

So churches of Christ plead for religious unity based upon the Bible. We believe that to subscribe to any creed other than the New Testament, to refuse to obey any New Testament command, or to follow any practice not sustained by the New Testament is to add to or take away from the teachings of God. And both additions and subtractions are condemned in the Bible (Galatians 1:6-9; Revelation 22:18,19). This is the reason the New Testament is the only rule of faith and practice we have in churches of Christ.

Each Congregation Self-Governed

Churches of Christ have none of the trappings of modern-day organizational bureaucracy. There are no governing boards – neither district, regional, national nor international – no earthly headquarters and no man-designed organization. Each congregation is autonomous (self- ruled) and is independent of every other congregation. The only tie which binds the many congregations together is a common allegiance to Christ and the Bible.

There are no conventions, annual meetings, nor official publications. Congregations do cooperate in supporting children's homes, homes for the elderly, mission work, etc. However, participation is strictly voluntary on the part of each congregation and no person nor group issues policies or makes decisions for other congregations. Each congregation is governed locally by a plurality of elders selected from among the members. These are men who meet the specific qualifications for this office given in 1 Timothy 3 and Titus 1.

There are also deacons in each congregation. These must meet the biblical qualifications of 1 Timothy 3. I

Items of Worship

Worship in churches of Christ centers in five items, the same as in the first-century church. We believe the pattern is important. Jesus said, "God is spirit, and those who worship Him must worship in spirit and truth" (John 4:24). From this statement we learn three things: 1) Our worship must be directed to the right object... God. 2) It must be prompted by the right spirit. 3) It must be according to truth.

To worship God according to truth is to worship Him according to His Word, because His Word is truth (John 17:17). Therefore, we must not exclude any item found in his Word, and we must not include any item not found in His Word. In matters of religion, we are to walk by faith (2 Corinthians 5:7). Since faith comes by hearing the Word of God (Romans 10:17), anything not authorized by the Bible cannot be done by faith... and whatever is not of faith is sin (Romans 14:23).

The five items of worship observed by the first-century church were singing, praying, preaching, giving, and eating the Lord's Supper. If you are acquainted with churches of Christ, you are probably aware that in two of these items our practice is different from that of most religious groups. So, permit me to focus on these two, and state our reasons for what we do.

A Cappella Singing

One of the things people most frequently notice about churches of Christ is that we sing without the use of mechanical instruments of music —a cappella singing is the only music used in our worship. Simply stated, here is the reason: we are seeking to worship according to the instructions of the New Testament. The New Testament leaves instrumental music out, therefore, we believe it right and safe to leave it out, too. If we used the mechanical instrument, we would have to do so without New Testament authority.

There are only eight verses in the New Testament on the subject of music in worship. Here they are:

> **Matthew 26:30**, "And when they had sung a hymn, they went out to the Mount of Olives"

> **Acts 16:25** "About midnight Paul and Silas were praying and singing hymns to God ..."

> **Romans 15:9** "Therefore I will praise Thee among the Gentiles, and sing to thy name"

> **1 Corinthians 14:15** ". . . I will sing with the spirit and I will sing with the mind also"

Ephesians 5:18,19 ". . . be filled with the Spirit, addressing one another in psalms and hymns and spiritual songs, singing and making melody to the Lord with all your heart"

Colossians 3:16 "Let the word of Christ dwell in you richly, as you teach and admonish one another in all wisdom, and as you sing psalms and hymns and spiritual songs with thankfulness in your hearts to God"

Hebrews 2:12 "I will declare thy name unto my brethren, in the midst of the church will I sing praise unto Thee"

James 5:13 "Is any one among you suffering? Let him pray. Is any cheerful? Let him sing praise"

The mechanical instrument of music is conspicuously absent in these passages. Historically, the first appearance of instrumental music in church worship was not until the sixth century A.D., and there was no general practicing of it until after the eighth century. Instrumental music was strongly opposed by such religious leaders as John Calvin, John Wesley, and Charles Spurgeon because of its absence in the New Testament.

Weekly Observance of The Lord's Supper

Another place where you may have noticed a difference between churches of Christ and other religious groups is in the Lord's Supper. This memorial supper was inaugurated by Jesus on the night of his betrayal (Matthew 26:26-28). It is observed by Christians in memory of the Lord's death (1 Corinthians 11:24,25). The emblems - unleavened bread and fruit of the vine - symbolize the body and blood of Jesus (1 Corinthians 10:16).

Churches of Christ are different from many in that we observe the Lord's Supper on the first day of every week. Again, our reason centers in our determination to follow the teaching of the New Testament. It says, describing the practice of the first-century church, "And upon the first day of the week...the disciples came together to break bread" (Acts 20:7).

Some have objected that the text does not specify the first day of every week. This is true – just as the command to observe the Sabbath did not specify every Sabbath. The command was simply, "Remember the Sabbath day to keep it holy" (Exodus 20:8). The Jews understood that to mean every Sabbath. It seems to us that by the same reasoning "the first day of the week" means the first day of every week.

Again, we know from such respected historians as Neander and Eusebius that Christians in those early centuries took the Lord's Supper every Sunday.

The Lord's church, the Church of Christ

Terms of Membership

Perhaps you are wondering, "How does one become a member of the church of Christ?" What are the terms of membership? Churches of Christ do not speak of membership in terms of some formula which must be followed for approved acceptance into the church. The New Testament gives certain steps which were taken by people in that day to become Christians. When a person became a Christian, he automatically was a member of the church. The same is true of churches of Christ today. There is no separate set of rules or ceremonies which one must follow to be inducted into the church. When one becomes a Christian, he, at the same time, becomes a member of the church. No further steps are required to qualify for church membership.

On the first day of the church's existence those who repented and were baptized were saved (Acts 2:38). And from that day forward all those who were saved were added to the church (Acts 2:47). According to this verse (Acts 2:47) it was God who did the adding. Therefore, in seeking to follow this pattern, we neither vote people into the church nor force them through a required series of studies. We have no right to demand anything beyond their obedient submission to the Savior.

The conditions of pardon which are taught in the New Testament are:
1) One must hear the gospel, for "faith comes by hearing the word of God" (Romans 10:17).
2) One must believe, for "without faith it is impossible to please God" (Hebrews 11:6).

3) One must repent of past sins, for God "commands all men, every- where to repent" (Acts 17:30).
4) One must confess Jesus as Lord, for he said, "He that confesses me before men, him will I also confess before my father who is in heaven" (Matthew 10:32).
5) And one must be baptized for the remission of sins, for Peter said, "Repent, and be baptized every- one of you in the name of Jesus Christ for the remission of your sins" (Acts 2:38).

Emphasis on Baptism

Churches of Christ have a reputation for placing much stress on the need for baptism. However, we do not emphasize baptism as a "church ordinance," but as a command of Christ. The New Testament teaches baptism as an act which is essential to salvation (Mark 16:16; Acts 2:38; Acts 22:16). We do not practice infant baptism because New Testament baptism is only for sinners who turn to the Lord in belief and penitence. An infant has no sin to repent of and cannot qualify as a believer.

The only form of baptism we practice in churches of Christ is immersion. The Greek word from which the word baptize comes means "to dip, to immerse, to sub- merge, to plunge." And the Scriptures always point to baptism as a burial (Acts 8:35-39; Romans 6:3,4; Colossians 2:12).

Baptism is extremely important because the New Testament sets forth the following purposes for it:
1) It is to enter the kingdom (John 3:5).
2) It is to contact Christ's blood (Romans 6:3,4).
3) It is to get into Christ (Galatians 3:27).
4) It is for salvation (Mark 16:16; 1 Peter 3:21).
5) It is for the remission of sins (Acts 2:38).
6) It is to wash away sins (Acts 22:16).
7) It is to get into the church (1 Corinthians 12:13; Ephesians 1:23).

Since Christ died for the sins of the whole world and the invitation to share in his saving grace is open to everyone (Acts 10:34,35; Revelation 22:17), we do not believe that anyone is predestined for salvation or condemnation. Some will choose to come to Christ in faith and obedience and will be saved. Others will reject his plea and be condemned (Mark 16:16). These will not be lost because they were marked for condemnation, but because that's the path they chose.

Wherever you are at this moment, we hope you will decide to accept the salvation offered by Christ - that you will offer yourself in obedient faith and become a member of his church.

In case you want further information on the church of Christ, I highly recommend you to watch the video of the World Video Bible School called *WHY ARE THERE SO MANY CHURCHES* on YouTube or reach out to The Gospel Broadcasting Network on YouTube or via E-mail (info@gbntv.org) or TheAuthenticChristian on Instagram.

If you want to find out more about the church of Christ you can do so by reading here: **https://church-of christ.org/who**

Chapter 6:
The New Age Movement

New Age is defined as, "A broad movement characterized by alternative approaches to traditional Western culture, with an interest in spirituality, mysticism, holism, and environmentalism." At first glance, this definition seems innocent enough. In fact, it even seems to be something that anyone striving for a healthy, stress-free life would be happy to participate in. There are many trappings of Western culture such as materialism, climbing the corporate ladder, over committing, social media pressure and the like that people long to be free of. What could be wrong with an alternative to Western cultural ideas that aren't healthy? Further, an interest in spirituality and a desire for the mystic are perceived as positive interests. Holism is taking into account the whole person or finding balance, another seemingly positive step towards healthy living. Finally, perhaps one of the most talked about ideas of the past decade, environmentalism. Caring for the environment is seen as a positive contribution to our world. When presented this way, New Age does not seem negative and in no way seems dangerous.

What is quickly overlooked in this definition is the "interest in spirituality and mysticism." Oftentimes, spirituality is used to speak of God and at times, so is mysticism. However, though both can accompany God, they are not exclusive to Him. Jesus says that He is the way, the truth, and the life. There are not multiple roads that lead to God. There are not multiple deities that can be explored to find the "god" that is right for you. Spirituality accompanies anything outside of ourselves, outside of the human spirit. Though many people would like to think this means positive energy, mother earth, an unknown higher power, or the power of self-actualization, the truth is that what exists in the spiritual world is God and His angels and Satan and his demons. Those are the only two categories.

Think about how little kids think. They believe in all types of what we call "imaginary" things. They believe whole-heartedly that the supernatural exists. They may say things like monsters and fairies, but could they be seeing into the spiritual realm? Could monsters be demons and fairies be angels but because we do not give them the appropriate language, they describe it as such? Somewhere along the way, children are told to no longer believe in things they may see and hear because it is only their imagination and adults insist that growing up means leaving these things behind. With it, we leave behind our innate insight into the spiritual realm. However, it still exists. Then as adults, when we start to struggle with spiritual forces, we call them things like bad energy, good vibes, intuition, deja vu and the like.

The Bible explains the two categories of the spiritual realm. In Ephesians, we learn about Satan's part in the spiritual realm. In chapter 2, Paul is speaking to the church at Ephesus, and he reminds them of where they came from. He says, "And you He made alive, who were dead in trespasses and sins, in which you once walked according to the course of this world, according to the prince of the power of the air, the spirit who now works in the sons of disobedience, among whom also we all once conducted ourselves in the lusts of our flesh, fulfilling the desires of the flesh and of the mind, and were by nature children of wrath, just as the others."

This explains that those who are influenced by this present age are influenced by Satan, the prince of the power of the air and that for anyone who does not believe in God, the spirit of Satan is already at work in them. This means that to be influenced by Satan, you do not have to be an overtly evil person or a gross sinner or desirer of evil, you simply need to be an unbeliever in God.

Further, in Ephesians chapter 6, Paul says, "For we do not wrestle against flesh and blood, but against principalities, against powers, against the rulers of the darkness of this age, against spiritual hosts of wickedness in the heavenly places." People often mistake all struggles as being "fleshly" or human. Anxiety, depression, fear, physical ailments, and in my case, even lack of sleep, have spiritual connections. We become so focused on the physical world that we do not acknowledge a spiritual realm.

The idea of mysticism, like spirituality, is subtle in its presentation but even more dangerous. Mysticism, though it can refer to experiencing God in the supernatural, rarely refers to God in His true character but more the idea of "a god." Mysticism refers to becoming one with God and refers to altered states of consciousness, no matter the cause, as mystical. Therefore, an altered state caused by drugs can be called mystical, an altered state caused by alcohol can be called mystical, an encounter with the true God can be called mystical, and an encounter with a demon can be called mystical. This generic term allows the individual to label any and all experiences as such blurring the lines between flesh and spirit.

Here in lies the issue, being part of the New Age Movement and embracing its philosophy opens you up to any type of non-human, non-earthly experience. In doing so, you invite in whatever is waiting for you and that means opening yourself to the satanic realm. If there are not large red flags, flashing danger signs, or overly harsh terminology people will go with the flow and not investigate for themselves the dangers involved. Just as in my simple pursuit for a sleep remedy, I was open to any experience, especially after hearing all about peace and angels from Jim. Because I was open to ANY experience, Satan and his demons were waiting for me.

Though the start of the New Age Movement cannot be narrowed down to a specific date, its ideas began in the counterculture of the 1960s and then grew in

The New Age Movement

the 1970's and developed into the 1980's. The movement was meant to bring love, light, and beauty for self. Here again, we see positive words and feelings associated with the movement, however, the Bible is clear that nothing good comes from worship of self.

In 1 Corinthians 10, Paul warns the reader by saying, "Therefore let him who thinks he stands take heed lest he fall...therefore my beloved, flee from idolatry." Later in 2 Timothy, Paul warns that there will come a day where, "Men will be lovers of themselves" and "lovers of pleasure rather than lovers of God." Psalm 10 tells us, "The wicked in his proud countenance does not seek God; God is in none of his thoughts." Proverbs 14:12 says, "There is a way that seems right to a man, but its end is the way of death." These verses do not reduce the love of God. His love for us is unconditional. These verses warn us of the results of pride when we place ourselves above God. In essence, that is what the New Age Movement does, it places the human spirit and human pursuits above God and in the end, its way is death.

This is what happened in the Garden of Eden when Adam and Eve sinned. They had all they needed. They had access to God. They had access to the Garden and food, the animals and each other. When Satan begins to talk to Eve, he uses ideas that are the same ideas of the modern New Age Movement. First, he does not act as if God does not exist. He acknowledges God when he asks Eve in Genesis 3, "Has God indeed said, 'You shall not eat of every tree of the garden?'" The New Age Movement acknowledges God or "gods" in any form. But what Satan does in his acknowledgement of

God is he takes the truth, and he twists it just subtly enough where it sounds like the truth.

When he quotes God, he misquotes Him. What God actually said was, "Of every tree of the garden you may freely eat; but of the tree of the knowledge of good and evil you shall not eat, for in the day that you eat of it you shall surely die. (Genesis 2:16-17)" Satan's misquote is an attempt to build a rapport with Eve. He wants her to know that he knows God and he knows what God said. He wants to build trust by bringing up something that seems innocent. The New Age Movement does the same. In my case, it was about getting more sleep. In other cases, it is about finding stress free options, clearing the mind, provoking positive energy, and loving the earth. All things that God would approve of in their right form but subtly twisted to place their pursuit above God exposing us to Satan, the Father of Lies.

Satan continues his deception of Eve when he uses his age-old lie on her. This is the same lie perpetrated throughout The New Age Movement. He says in Genesis 3, "You will not surely die. For God knows that in the day you eat of it your eyes will be opened, and you will be like God, knowing good and evil." In this one statement, he assures Eve that there are no consequences to disobeying God and that when she does, she will be a "god" herself.

One of the tenants of the New Age Movement is the emphasis on the individual and the individual's experiences becoming their own spirituality. In essence, becoming a god ourselves. This is self-worship, self-worship is idol worship, and idol worship is a tactic of Satan. As Riaan Engelbrecht states in his book *Perilous Times S Vol 5: Darkness Descends*, "Satan has been hard at work to exalt man in his own eyes, and at the same time, to reduce the divinity of God to a state of no longer being the Creator of all but being part of Creation's natural evolution."

In Matthew 4, Satan tries to use this tactic on Jesus himself. It says, "Again, the devil took Him up on an exceedingly high mountain, and showed Him all the kingdoms of the world and their glory. And he said to Him, all these things I will give You if You fall down and worship me. Then Jesus said to him, away with you, Satan! For it is written, 'You shall worship the Lord your God, and Him only you shall serve.'" When an individual participates in New Age, whether they truly understand it or not, they are opening themselves up to Satan because New Age itself is based on his lies.

Studies done by Pew Research Center show that The New Age Movement appeals to a wide variety of people because it is for those who claim to be religious but not spiritual, spiritual but not religious, and both spiritual and religious. (Gecewicz, Claire. "'New Age' Beliefs Common among Both Religious and Nonreligious Americans." Pew Research Center. Pew Research Center, August 27, 2020. https://www.pewresearch.org/fact-tank/2018/10/01/new-age-beliefs-common-among-both-religious-and-nonreligious-americans/.) Though identifying with traditional religious titles such as Catholic or Protestant can come with preconceived ideas and judgment, identifying as New Age seems to be acceptable to most. This is because New Age promotes itself as an all-inclusive, come as you are, believe what you want type of "religion." However, when we dive deeper into the New Age Movement, beyond the surface and shallow façade, we see the multi-faceted beliefs system based on Gnosticism.

Delving into the understanding of Gnosticism can produce more confusion than clarity. There are thousands of explanations of the start and development of Gnosticism, and each has its own variation of what the belief system entails. The root word "gnosis" means knowledge. The word "gnostic" describes mysterious intellectual or spiritual knowledge. "Gnosticism" describes the thought and practice of various cults that matter is evil, and freedom comes through "gnosis," which is knowledge of spiritual truth. Essentially, salvation, enlightenment, or oneness with God could be reached through an understanding or special knowledge. That understanding is that the Creator God is evil, making all created matter evil, and Jesus is good and in turn made the human spirit good. In other words, God = Evil, Humans = Good. This is the very opposite of the Gospel. The Gospel is clear that God is a good, loving Father and humans are as Jeremiah 17:9 tells us "The heart *is* deceitful above all *things,* And desperately wicked; Who can know it?"

It was this belief of the Gnostics that humans could in fact be their own savior, their own deliverer, enlighten themselves, and eventually become "godlike" or one with God that began to grow exponentially.

The idea of Gnosticism takes us right back to the story of Eve's and Satan's conversation in the Garden of Eden. Satan convinced Eve that there was special knowledge and that the special knowledge, when consumed, would make her like God. In doing so, he called God a liar and implied that God's reason for not wanting her to eat from the tree was because of jealousy (not wanting Eve to be like Him) making God evil and the human spirit good. Gnosticism is simply the same deception of Satan wrapped up in a different package.

Gnosticism began in the Christian church in the second century. Christian philosophers began to look for a better means or explanation of redemption and in doing so looked to apostles of Jesus for a special revelation that would hold the key to salvation. Jesus had already explained the key to salvation and his apostles and disciples explained the key as well. There was no special knowledge needed. Ephesians 2:8-9 states, "For by grace you have been saved through faith, and that not of yourselves; it is a gift of God." 2 Corinthians 5:21 tells us, "For He made Him who knew no sin to be sin for us, that we might become the righteousness of God in Him."

In Acts 16, the Jailer asks Paul and Silas what he must do to be saved and they reply, "Believe on the Lord Jesus Christ, and you will be saved, you and your household. Then they spoke the word of the Lord to him and to all who were in his house. And he took them the same hour of the night and washed their stripes. And immediately he and all his family were baptized." The key had already been given. The truth had already been told, just as God had told the truth to Adam in the garden in Genesis 3, "And the Lord God commanded the man, saying, 'Of every tree of the garden you may freely eat; but of the tree of knowledge of good and evil you shall not eat for in the day that you eat of it you shall surely die.'" Gnosticism in turn grew out of the prideful thought that salvation, given freely as a gift of God with no work of mankind required, must not be that simple. There must be more to it that involves the thoughts and efforts and workings of mankind because mankind is so important and good. This morphed into the idea that salvation, enlightenment, and redemption could be achieved by man alone. God was not required. Satan's perfect deception and the perfect open door for what would become the New Age Movement.

The main beliefs of the New Age Movement are polar opposite of Christianity. The first main belief is that God is in everything. This is known as Pantheism. Pantheism is explained as God is the universe and the universe is God. Pantheism promotes the idea that God is not a personal God with any interest in the lives of mankind, but instead God is all the laws, forces, and elements of the universe. God is the wind. God is the sun. God is gravity. God is a galaxy. God is a feeling.

Paul speaks about this in Romans 1:20-22 when he is talking about mankind exchanging the truth for unrighteousness. He says, "For since the creation of the world His invisible *attributes* are clearly seen, being understood by the things that are made, *even* His eternal power and Godhead, so that they are without excuse, because, although they knew God, they did not glorify *Him* as God, nor were thankful, but became futile in their thoughts, and their foolish hearts were darkened. Professing to be wise, they became fools, and changed the glory of the incorruptible God into an image made like corruptible man—and birds and four-footed animals and creeping things…they exchanged the truth of God for the lie and worshiped and served the creature rather than the Creator, who is blessed forever."

Countless religions and practices around the world in the past and present have turned something God created into the item to be worshipped instead of worshipping the Creator Himself. This is Pantheism, and the first main belief of New Age. The very story of Satan's fall from heaven was that he, the created thing, wanted to be worshipped instead of worshipping the Creator. He has since deceived mankind to worship idols of all kinds but mainly the idol of self-worship. The worship of humanity over the worship of God leads individuals directly into Satan's grasp.

Christianity promotes, believes, and ascribes to the worship of God and God alone. Psalm 96 proclaims, "For the Lord *is* great and greatly to be praised; He *is* to be feared above all gods. For all the gods of the peoples *are* idols, But the Lord made the heavens. Honor and majesty *are* before Him; Strength and beauty *are* in His sanctuary." Philippians 2 states, "At the name of Jesus every knee should bow, of those in heaven, and of those on earth, and of those under the earth, and that every tongue should confess that Jesus Christ is Lord, to the glory of God the Father." In Exodus 20, we find what has come to be known as the Ten Commandments. The first commandment states, "You shall have no other gods before Me." Again, we see Satan's influence on the New Age Movement as this idea of Pantheism violates the Word of God. Just as Satan tried to get Eve to worship herself and tried to tempt Jesus Himself to bow down in worship, Satan subtly uses this first belief of New Age, to make the true God something that is unnecessary and open for any interpretation mankind gives to Him.

The second main belief of the New Age Movement is that all things are one. This is known as Monism. Monism is a version of Pantheism though based on the words themselves it does not seem so. Pan means "many" and Mono means "one" so how can the two words mean virtually the same thing? Remember that Pantheism ascribes that God is in everything and everything is in God. Monism ascribes that there is only one substance and there is no distinction between substances such as matter and mind, or God and the world because only one substance exists. In essence, God is the world, and the world is God. This leads right back to Pantheism and the lies of Satan. However, Monism takes it a step further.

Monism believes that the one substance that exists is neutral. This means that only physical things exist like trees, air, and the body. Because everything comes from one substance, everything is neutral. There is nothing more special about a human than there is about a tree. They both have the same substance. There is no soul or other abstract quality ascribed to humans. Monism removes the very God given trait that makes humans in fact, special, being made in the image of God.

In Genesis 2:7, when God is creating Adam it says, "And the Lord God formed man of the dust of the ground, and breathed into his nostrils the breath of life; and man became a living being." It further says in Genesis 1, "So God created man in His own image; in the image of God, He created him; male and female He created them." Humans are indeed different from any other substance on earth. Humans were made in the image of God and God breathed the breath of life into them. They are made of spirit, soul, and body, three distinct parts of man. Ultimately, Monism, attempts to strip God of His creative power and to remove the need for salvation. Whereas Pantheism gives individuals the path to save themselves, Monism eliminates the need for a path at all. If fully ascribing to Monism, there is no one to live for other than self because there is no soul, and nothing abstract such as feelings and conscience. Those who ascribe to this New Age belief only have to care about self and what pleases self. In Essence, self-worship. We can see again that Satan has no new ideas and tactics.

The third main belief of the New Age Movement is the idea that the mind creates reality and truth. It is true that a person's perceptions help to create their reality. Proverbs warns of this in chapter 23, "For as he [man] thinks in his heart, so is he." However, the true danger of this New Age belief is that it allows for truth to be based on a person's reality or concept of reality. Basically, what is true for me, is the ultimate truth and what is true for you is the ultimate truth. On a smaller scale, this is not disruptive to the spiritual nature of our lives. For example, if a child is bitten by a dog and the reaction of his parent is to keep him from all dogs because "dogs are vicious," he will grow up with his reality being "dogs are vicious." Another child can grow up with dogs in their home that are part of the family and loving companions, this child will grow up with his reality being "dogs are loving." Both children would be correct. Dogs can be vicious, and dogs can be loving, but their reality is based on their experience.

Our experiences and our perceptions add to our reality but there are ultimate truths that do not change. Scenario A: If you are to grow up only surrounded by goodness and love, evil still exists. Scenario B: If you are to grow up only surrounded by evil, goodness and love still exists. What the concept of "mind created reality and truth" does is it says that for the individual in scenario A, evil does not exist and for the individual in scenario B, goodness and love do not exist. The danger is that when the reality of evil hits the one who does not believe it exists the foundation of their life is shaken. The same holds true when love hits the one who does not believe it exists.

In contrast, Jesus provides an unshakable, ultimate truth. One of the most quoted verses in the Bible is John 8:32, "You shall know the truth, and the truth shall make you free." But oftentimes, the verse is not explained in its context or to its fullness. Jesus had been speaking to Jews and in this particular verse, He is speaking to Jews who believed that He was God. The whole verse reads, "If you abide in My word, you are My disciples indeed. And you shall know the truth, and truth shall make you free." The Jews who were hearing this for the first time were confused. They did not understand what it was they needed to be set free from. They asked Jesus for a better explanation because in their opinion, as Abraham's descendants, they had never been in bondage to anyone. "Jesus answered them, 'Most assuredly, I say to you, whoever commits sin is a slave of sin. And a slave does not abide in the house forever, but a son abides forever. Therefore, if the Son makes you free, you shall be free indeed.'" John 8:34

There is ultimate truth that can be known, and it is known by abiding in Christ Jesus and in His Word, the Bible. However, the truth cannot be known until you are set free from and leave the slavery of sin to become a son or daughter of God. By ascribing to the teaching that truth is different for everyone and is only based on the mind and individual experiences, the ascribed denies the ultimate truth of Freedom in Christ and Freedom from Sin.

Satan told Eve to believe that her reality, wanting to eat the delicious looking fruit, was her truth. He told Judas to believe that his reality, wanting money and recognition, was his truth. The TRUTH about Satan is told by Jesus in John 8 when he says, "He [Satan] was a murderer from the beginning, and does not stand in the truth, because there is no truth in him. When he speaks a lie, he speaks from his own resources, for he is a liar and the father of it." Again, we see Satan using this main belief of the New Age Movement to encourage people to rewrite the truth into a lie and to accept that lie as truth. In doing so, he separates the individual from seeking the truth of Jesus and His Word and again, eliminates the need for God.

The fourth main belief of the New Age Movement is Syncretism. Syncretism is the combing of different beliefs, while blending various practices. This is where many Eastern Religions come into play. Though many in the New Age Movement claim that New Age is not a religion rather a mindset, the movement itself incorporates many Eastern religions such as Hinduism, Buddhism, Taoism, and Confucianism. Each of these religions, in and off themselves practices a certain level of syncretism. These religions along with New Age, allow followers to pick and choose what they want and want they don't want. You can choose the suffering path of the Buddhist, the belief in a Hindu god along with a belief in Jesus, the "humanity follows the earth" belief of Taoism, and the Silver Rule of Behavior of Confucianism all while not jeopardizing the state of your eternal soul.

Syncretism is truly the foundation of New Age. All must be accepted for Gnosticism, Pantheism, Monism, and mind reality to be accepted. New Age claims to seek peace, enlightenment, and a rising above of sorts. This rising above is often touted as a rising above religious oppression. New Age will state that Christianity is an overbearing, rule heavy, exclusive, oppressive religion while New Age is a burden free, follow your own rules, inclusive, free, non-religious movement. The New Age description of Christianity shows a complete lack of understanding of the Word of God or the love of Jesus. Christianity, when presented as a religion, can become overbearing as any religion can be, but when presented as the loving relationship with Jesus that it truly is, Christianity is a path to freedom from sin and is inclusive, as "whosoever calls on the name of the Lord shall be saved." Salvation is for anyone who follows these steps:

> *Hear* the gospel Romans 10:17
>
> *Believe* the gospel John 3:16
>
> *Repent* Luke 13:3
>
> *Confess* Jesus as Savior and Lord Romans 10:9
>
> *Be immersed in water and added to the church* Acts 2:36-47, 22:16, 1 Peter 3:21
>
> *Be faithful unto death* Revelation 2:10, Philippians 2:12

By making anything holy, nothing is holy. Here again, Satan twists the truth, masquerading as an angel of light presenting a seemingly harmless, peace-filled outlook on life. However, any step into the New Age Movement is a step into the control of Satan. When I chose to speak the shaman ritual over my home and my life it was a seemingly innocent step towards peace and rest, but the consequences of believing Satan's deception had disastrous effects on me. I am wheelchair bound for the rest of my life because I took The New Age Movement lightly and did not consider how dangerous it is. Satan is our enemy. He is a lion seeking whom he may devour, and we must be vigilant when it comes to the tactics he uses.

Chapter 7:
Yoga

Yoga is a popular practice today and is hailed as a unique and beneficial exercise program. Yoga promotes health and wellness along with increasing oxygen intake and creating a relaxed atmosphere. But is this all there is to yoga? Many may be surprised to find out that when you practice yoga, you are practicing a physical, mental, and spiritual discipline that is one of the six orthodox schools of the philosophy of Hinduism. At the beginning of the development of Hinduism, when religious writings were being established as canonical texts, the practice of Yoga was written as a spiritual discipline paying homage to the many Hindu gods.

The term has been shortened to be referred to as "Yoga," but it is actually called Yoga Sutra. A sutra is a rule or a thought that is part of Hindu holy literature. That means that these poses represent spiritual ideals of the Hindu religion. For example, the Warrior Poses are taken from a story about Virabhadra who is a form of the Hindu god Shiva. Shiva is one of the main deities of the Hindu religion and is also called the Great

Lord and Great God. Shiva is believed to be half male and half female as well as half evil and half good. He can poison someone as well as heal them. He can care for human souls or slaughter them. He has power over snakes and can compel them to do his bidding. Many people will say that the Warrior Poses are innocent and can simply be applied to having confidence in yourself and conquering what is in front of you. However, the spiritual meaning and evilness tied to them still remains. There is only one Great God and Great Lord and that is God the Father. The God of the Bible. The God who is not consumed with both love and destruction and who is not both good and evil. He is a God of love, and He alone is worthy of worship.

The spiritual meaning of poses does not end with Shiva. The Child's Pose represents surrendering oneself to the earth goddess, Bhumi. This pose is taught as innocent and peaceful. However, the tribute to Bhumi is one of worship. The pose requires the poser to kneel, placing their lower torso between their knees, extending arms alongside the torso with palms facing down. It is a complete bowing down. It is called the Child's Pose because Bhumi gave birth to a child who made a deal with spirits that only Bhumi could kill him. Living with this assurance, he captured 16,000 women making them his wives by force. The only solution was for his mother, Bhumi to kill him. This is what is being paid homage to with the Child's Pose.

The Tree Pose is based on a story about the demon king Ravana. The Anjali Mudra Poses, the most common pose, is a pose of prayer to the gods of Hindu. The beginning pose of many Yoga sessions is Sun

Salutation Pose. It is promoted as a pose for opening up breathing, but the pose is meant to celebrate the sun-god, Surya. The list goes on and on. Yoga is not simply exercise used for stretching and breathing. It is a spiritual discipline of Hinduism.

Plainly stated, Yoga is idolatry because it is worship of other gods. Every pose and aspect of Yoga was created as a tribute to or as a way to connect to a Hindu god. However, some accept a watered-down version of Yoga as exercise that increases flexibility, peace, and breathing. Even with this thought pattern Yoga, at best, is pantheism. Pantheism is the belief that God is in everything, and everything is in God. It is a type of worship that tolerates and accepts all other gods. Those who promote Yoga as simple meditation and becoming one with yourself are promoting pantheism in its most basic form.

Christians are called to live their lives as it says in Colossians 3:17, "And whatever you do in word or deed, do all in the name of the Lord Jesus, giving thanks to God the Father through Him." One cannot participate in Yoga in the name of the Lord Jesus. There are "Christian" yoga studios that play worship music and pray before and after each session believing this will remove any aspects of other religions, but does this remove the ties to false religion and evil spirits? It does not! Isaiah 5:20 says, "Woe to those who call evil good, and good evil; Who put darkness for light, and light for darkness; Who put bitter for sweet, and sweet for bitter!"

When Jesus is speaking to the women at the well in the book of John, He is explaining to her that she may worship but she does not know or understand the worship. In chapter 4:22-24 He says, "You worship what you do not know; we know what we worship, for salvation is of the Jews. But the hour is coming, and now is, when the true worshipers will worship the Father in spirit and truth; for the Father is seeking such to worship Him. God *is* Spirit, and those who worship Him must worship in spirit and truth." Believers and unbelievers alike have the truth available to them in the Word of God. Believers are to worship God and Him alone in spirit and in truth. Meaning, we are to seek out the truth and apply it to our lives. The truth of Yoga is that it is a religious practice. It is worship of false gods. False gods are a doorway to the demonic. Worshipping false gods is idolatry.

This may seem harsh for something that is promoted as simple exercise and healthy lifestyle. However, Paul is clear in Galatians 1:8-9 when he says, "But even if we, or an angel from heaven, preach any other gospel to you than what we have preached to you, let him be accursed. As we have said before, so now I say again, if anyone preaches any other gospel to you than what you have received, let him be accursed." Yoga is another gospel. It is part of the gospel of Hinduism and those who practice it participate in the worship it entails. As we have previously discussed, Satan is often subtle in the way he exposes us to things that are contrary to God. Just as he posed the question to Eve, "Has God indeed said?" He says things like, "Did God really say you shouldn't do it? Is it really that bad? It's just exercise. Don't you feel better after? You should be proud of yourself for getting healthy. Yoga is simply exercise." And on he goes with his many deceptions. We must capture every thought and make it subject to God by reading the Word of God, the Bible. His Word is clear that we are to worship Him alone. Do not be deceived by Yoga as it is innocently presented. Be on guard against the wiles of Satan who is the Father of Lies.

And no wonder! For Satan himself transforms himself into an angel of light. (2 Corinthians 11:14)

Chapter 8:
Occultism

What comes to mind when you hear the word "occult?" Is it rituals? Satanic activity? Or is it like New Age and Astrology, cloaked in innocence or even ignorance? Most people will believe that they have more knowledge or experience with New Age and Astrology than they do with the occult, but when we break down what occultism really is, we see that it has permeated our world.

The occult refers to any hidden supernatural, mystical, or magical beliefs, practices, or phenomena. It comes from a Latin word meaning hidden or obscured. For example, during an eclipse, it is said that one celestial body occults, or hides another. By the very definition, occultism is something that is hidden so how do we learn about something that is hidden? Luke 12:2 tells us, "For there is nothing covered that will not be revealed, nor hidden that will not be known." Ecclesiastes 12:14 says, "For God will bring every work into judgment, including every secret thing, whether good or evil." As much as Satan, the deceiver, tries to hide himself and his agenda, God reveals his tactics and plans.

Occultism begins with a belief in the supernatural. This belief can be found in virtually every society throughout written history. This is because the supernatural IS real. As stated previously, there are two realms within the supernatural, the heavenly realm and the demonic realm. However, to acknowledge this is to acknowledge that God and Satan both exist and that they are active in this present world. The deception of occultism is that the supernatural can be acknowledged, without acknowledging God or Satan. 1 John 5:19 speaking of Satan says, "The whole world lies under the sway of the wicked one." Occultism is perhaps the most dangerous of deceptions by Satan because it opens the door to the supernatural without acknowledging the existence of God or Satan. In this dangerous place, people interact with the supernatural realm without truly understanding they are being deceived. The world has become comfortable with speaking about magic, divination, witchcraft, and the like all of which are part of the demonic realm but are rarely acknowledged as such. There are movies, games, cartoons, television shows, and toys that embrace occultism by making it a playful, magical experience instead of acknowledging its roots.

The roots of occultism are Hellenistic. The Hellenistic Period was between 323 BC and 31 BC. It was a time where devotion to Greek culture, style, and civilization was strong. This time period saw an increase in Hellenism which is a polytheistic religion believing in many gods including Greek gods such as Zeus, Poseidon, and Hermes. A form of Christian Hellenism developed as well that mixed some practices of traditional Christianity with Hellenistic ideas. Out of this, the "mysterious" secret philosophies were acknowledged and "hidden" things such as spirits, black magic, and the like were acknowledged and practiced. It was also a time where alchemy was being developed by the Greeks. Alchemy was the beginning of chemistry, but with the lack of understanding of how elements worked, alchemy was a seemingly magical process of transformation, creation, and combination of elements to create secret elixirs to heal and transform.

During this time, Jewish mysticism was also growing. There was a doctrine of a secret, mystical interpretation of the Torah called the Kabbala. These two things, Jewish mysticism and Hellenistic alchemy and philosophy, came together to create Hermeticism. Hermeticism took both the practice of magic "for good" and some elements of Jewish theology and paired them together creating occultism, which was presented as a good, natural magic.

As Hermeticism grew, it evolved into different sects such as Spiritualism: communication between the spiritual world and natural world and Theosophy: a blend of occultism and mysticism which allowed for humans to become mediums for the spiritual world to pass into the natural world. As the understanding of chemistry grew and as philosophy emerged as a study of the natural world, occult practices seemed to die down.

How does this tie into modern times? What does modern occultism look like? In a sense, anyone who wants to figure out the mysterious of the universe and how the universe works steps into occultism because in its basic form it is a study of the "hidden" and "mysterious". The mystery of the universe, creation, and how things came to be is something that has permeated generations. We, as humans, want to know why and how. We are driven by the need for purpose that was created in us by God. When God is removed from the equation, humans do not know their purpose and seek it out in ways that seem right to them. Deuteronomy 29:29 tells us, "The secret things belong to the Lord our God." The mysteries and hidden things of the universe belong to God but in Jeremiah, we learn that if we seek Him, He will reveal these things to us. Jeremiah 33:3 says, "Call to Me, and I will answer you, and show you great and mighty things, which you do not know."

Further, in the New Testament we learn that the great mysteries have been revealed to us as Believers. In Colossians 2:1-3, Paul is speaking about believers, and he desires for them to understand, "That their hearts may be encouraged, being knit together in love, and attaining to all riches of the full assurance of understanding, to the knowledge of the mystery of God, both of the Father and of Christ, in whom are hidden all the treasures of wisdom and knowledge." In Christ, we have all we need. However, occultism removes God from the picture, does not acknowledge the truth of the spiritual realm, and promotes solving the mysteries of the universe and human existence by seeking a version of the supernatural that seems harmless. God has revealed these sought-after mysteries through creation and through Christ. Once we believe, our eyes are opened, and we turn from these things towards Christ. We then begin to speak the truth to those who do not believe. 2 Corinthians 4:2-4 says, "But we have renounced the hidden things of shame, not walking in craftiness nor handling the word of God deceitfully, but by manifestation of the truth commending ourselves to every man's conscience in the sight of God. But even if our gospel is veiled, it is veiled to those who are perishing, whose minds the god (Satan) of this age has blinded, who do not believe, lest the light of the gospel of the glory of Christ, who is the image of God, should shine on them."

This verse tells us that Satan, "the god of this age," has blinded the eyes of those who do not believe. He blinds them by taking some truth and mixing it with lies. Remember, this is the same tactic he used in the Garden of Eden. Though his methods may change, his tactics do not. Satan is not creative. Creativity alone belongs to God and those who were made in His image. With occultism, he takes the truth that the supernatural does exist and that humans long to know the mysterious but he mixes it with the lie that pursuit of the mysterious through occultism is harmless, fun even.

The Ouija Board is sold as a family board game. Though it may seem like a recent invention, it was actually created in 1890. It is a wooden board with the letters of the alphabet, numbers, and the words "yes," "no," and "goodbye." It comes with a teardrop shaped device with a small window. Two or more players are supposed to put their fingers on the device, ask it a question, and wait for the device to move spelling out an answer. It seems innocent enough, right? Not exactly. The board was developed during a time when Spiritualism (communicating with the spiritual realm) was growing in America. Not only was it growing, but it did not seem to cause problems for those who claimed to be Christians. Since the Christian church taught the existence of the spiritual realm, it seems completely acceptable to speak to that realm and seek answers. One reason Spiritualism was growing at this time was because many people died young. Women in childbirth, children in sickness, and young men in the Civil War all died before their time. People wanted to speak to their loved ones "beyond the grave."

The name Ouija is said to have come from the board itself. A medium sat at the board and asked what it should be called, and the board responded by moving the teardrop device to spell out O-u-i-j-a. When asked what that meant, the board spelled "good luck." Over the years, there have been many headlines about people who were told to do something from the board such as committing crimes and murders and in the last forty years it has been shown in many paranormal movies and tv shows. But psychologist say it's all fun and games. Our minds play tricks on us and cause us to push the teardrop device even though we swear we are not moving it. What a powerful tool of the Enemy this is!

The Ouija Board is just one of MANY ways that occultism enters homes and families. Anyone can do a quick google search and find the twenty-five best movies and tv shows about witches for kids and families. From cartoons to kid's shows, to family movies, being a witch, wizard, or sorcerer is being portrayed as funny and harmless. But is it really harmless? Witches, sorcerers, and those who practice divination are real. They operate under the control of the demonic realm. They may come across as peaceful and good, but the Bible tells us that even Satan appears as an angel of light (2. Corinthians 11:14). Witches, sorcerers, and wizards have no place in our lives. When we engage with them or seek out their counsel, we invite the demonic into our lives. When children learn through tv shows and cartoons that witchcraft is funny and innocent, they become open to accepting in into their lives in the future.

When God was establishing laws for the Israelites in the Old Testament, He knew they would be living among and around pagan cultures. Though we often think of modern times as being more open to occultism, it was present during Biblical times as well because Satan is the perpetrator of the occult. In establishing the laws for His followers, God says in Leviticus 19:31, "Give no regard to mediums and familiar spirits; do not seek after them, to be defiled by them: I am the Lord your God." Leviticus 20:6 says, "And the person who turns to mediums and familiar spirits, to prostitute himself with them, I will set my face against that person…" In Isaiah chapter 8, Isaiah is speaking about the influence of pagans on God's people. He says in verses 19-20, "And when they say to you, 'Seek those who are mediums and wizards, who whisper and mutter, 'Should not a people seek their God? Should they seek the dead on behalf of the living?' To the law and to the testimony! If they do not speak according to the word, it is because there is no light in them.'"

He makes it very clear that unless someone is speaking the truth of the Word of God, the light is not in them. There are many more scriptures in the Old Testament that speak to those who practice the occult (Exodus 22:18, Leviticus 21:8, I Samuel 15:23, 2 Chronicles 33:6, Deuteronomy 19:9-22, 18:10, Leviticus 19:26).

Some may say that we are under the New Covenant and that the Old Testament laws do not apply to us today. However, the New Testament provides even harsher warnings to those who practice occultism. Revelation 21:8 says, "But the cowardly, unbelieving, abominable, murderers, sexually immoral, sorcerers, idolaters, and all liars shall have their part in the lake which burns with fire and brimstone, which is the second death." Galatians 5:19-21 says, " Now the works of the flesh are evident, which are: adultery, fornication, uncleanness, lewdness, idolatry, sorcery, hatred, contentions, jealousies, outbursts of wrath, selfish ambitions, dissensions, heresies, envy, murders, drunkenness, revelries, and the like; of which I tell you beforehand, just as I also told *you* in time past, that those who practice such things will not inherit the kingdom of God." These verses are difficult to read because they are very firm in the destiny of those we participate in such things. But it is important to hear these verses. The Word of God is living and active and for anyone involved in witchcraft (sorcery) or any other form of occultism hearing these verses can bring about repentance and deliverance from these acts of Satan.

Modern day witches often practice it, in the form of psychics. Psychics present an option for those who need direction. Using fortune telling through tarot cards, palm reading, crystals, auras, or energy they claim to know the right path in finances, relationships, careers, family, and more. Going in for a palm reading, having tarot cards read to us, or seeking life direction seems innocent or fun but these individuals derive their "powers" from Satan and visiting a psychic opens the door to the demonic realm. Again, psychics seek to explain things to you that can only be explained by God and a relationship with Jesus. They are in essence taking the place of God creating a type of idolatry.

Psychics can have knowledge and power to speak things that are true. This is because fortune telling is done through the spirit of divination. Acts 16:16-17 tells the account of one girl that was possessed by the spirit of divination. It reads, "Now it happened, as we went to prayer, that a certain slave girl possessed with a spirit of divination met us, who brought her masters much profit by fortune-telling. This girl followed Paul and us, and cried out, saying, 'These men are the servants of the Most High God, who proclaim to us the way of salvation.' And this she did for many days. But Paul, greatly annoyed, turned and said to the spirit, 'I command you in the name of Jesus Christ to come out of her.'" And he came out that very hour.'"

The "spirit of divination" is translated from the Greek word Pythonos, which literally means "a spirit of Python." During the time of Acts in Delphi (southern Greece) there was a serpent named Python. Those who lived in Delphi said that Python had the power of divination. Once again, we return to the Garden of Eden where Satan spoke through a serpent to deceive

Eve and predict the future. Remember in Genesis 3:4 when Eve is deciding if she will eat the forbidden fruit that God has said will lead to death, Satan says, "You will not surely die." He, in a sense, is fortune telling. He is telling Eve what she wants to hear so she can do what she wants to do. His prediction seems good. His predication seems right. His prediction seems to solidify Eve's decision, but his prediction led to death. This is always the path that Satan will create for us, one of death, theft, and destruction (John 10:10). Any practice within the occult is joining his side and allowing him the open door to control you. As I have previously mentioned, I was not thinking of Satan or the demonic realm in any way when I conducted the shaman ritual, but Satan will go through any open door whether it is intentionally opened or not. "Be sober, be vigilant; because your adversary the devil walks about like a roaring lion, seeking whom he may devour" (1 Peter 5:8).

Chapter 9:
Law of Attraction (Manifesting)

The word manifesting can have many different meanings. Here, we want to understand it in the context of spirituality. What is manifesting and how is it contrary to what the Bible teaches? Manifesting, in the spiritual sense, is the belief that through enough positive thoughts, meditation on wanted outcomes, and spoken mantras, your desires, wants, and dreams can come true. For example, if you want to manifest a house think about it, meditate on it, say over and over, "I will have a house" and eventually you will have a house. This is more commonly referred to as the law of attraction.

The law of attraction is the belief that the magnetic pull of the universe through people, objects, thoughts, and desires can bring you what you want. Positive thoughts bring about positive results. Negative thoughts bring about negative results. This is a philosophy, like astrology, that is built on pseudoscience. It is the belief that if you think it enough, you will manifest it in your life.

The history of the law of attraction has its origins in Buddhism. Buddha is quoted as saying, "All that we are is a result of what we have thought." As time progressed, this mantra of Buddhism was used to create the idea of the law of attraction. By the 19th century, the philosophy was in full force. Helena Balvastsky travelled throughout the world promoting the belief in manifesting through the law of attraction. She is quoted as saying, "The Universe is worked and guided from within outwards" ("Helena Petrovna Blavatsky Quotes (Author of The Secret Doctrine)." Goodreads. Goodreads. Accessed July 1, 2021. https://www.goodreads.com/author/quotes/18295027.Helena_Petrovna_Blavatsky.).

In the early 20th century, William Atkinson promoted the law of attraction as being strengthen through willpower. He said, "Permit each man to think according to his light" (Admin. "Law of Attraction." SoigsiOnline, April 25, 2021. http://soigsi.online/law-o-f-attraction/.).

Ester Hicks, another proponent of manifestation in the 20th century, promoted it as a means of healing. She said, "You have the power to heal your life, and you need to know that" ("Louise L. Hay Quotes (Author of You Can Heal Your Life)." Goodreads. Goodreads. Accessed July 1, 2021. https://www.goodreads.com/author/quotes/74538.Louise_L_Hay.).

The 21st Century saw a surge in the law of attraction with the book *The Secret* being released in 2006. This widely successful book that was made into a movie promotes the idea that the universe receives the energy of your thoughts. If you think what you want, it will come to you. If you complain about what you don't have you will not receive it. *The Secret* claims, "The law of attraction is the greatest and most infallible law upon which the entire system of creation depends." This statement is in direct contradiction of God's Word. The "greatest and most infallible" foundation is the love of God demonstrated through the sacrifice of His one and only Son, Jesus Christ. Romans 5:8 says, "God demonstrates His own love toward us, in that while we were still sinners, Christ died for us." The "entire system of creation" is built on this foundation and this foundation alone. Believing that the law of attraction serves this purpose is a lie. The law of attraction and manifestation are tricks of the Enemy born out of his desire to deceive.

As we have discussed, Satan takes Biblical truths and twists them just slightly, so they seem harmless when really, they are detrimental to the whole understanding of God's Kingdom. This is what has happened with the law of attraction. There are proponents of this law that say it is a law that Jesus taught. They use Scripture out of context to try to show this. Let's look at four of the main beliefs of the law of attraction and how these beliefs twist the truth.

The law of attraction says, "Everything starts with your thinking". Proverbs 23:7 says, "For as a man thinks in his heart, so is he." Many say that this is the same principle so it must be Biblical. However, this verse is taken out of context. It is really talking about deception. In context the verse reads, "Do not eat the bread of a miser, nor desire his delicacies; For as he thinks in his heart, so *is* he. "Eat and drink!" he says to you, but his heart is not with you." This verse is about a greedy person saying one thing with his mouth when he really feels the opposite. It has nothing to do with manifesting through thinking.

Now, there is a lot the Bible does say about your thinking effecting your life. Colossians 3:2 says, "Set your mind on things above, not on things on the earth" but the law of attraction says to set you mind on the things of this earth, material possessions, and worldly success. The Bible tells us in Matthew 6:33 to, "Seek first the kingdom of God and His righteousness, and all these things shall be added to you." Our thinking should be on God, our Creator. He only is the answer. Our desire should be for His will and His will alone. We should put our desires aside and seek His will. Romans 12:2 says, "Do not be conformed to this world, but be transformed by the renewing of your mind, that you may prove what *is* that good and acceptable and perfect will of God." God's will is what we should focus our thinking on. You see, our minds are the battleground for spiritual warfare. 2 Corinthians 10:4-5 says, "For the weapons of our warfare *are* not carnal but mighty in God for pulling down strongholds, casting down arguments and every high thing that exalts itself against the knowledge of God, bringing every thought into captivity to the obedience of Christ." The principle of the law of attraction that teaches "our thoughts are the beginning of all we could want or desire" is contrary to Scripture. A relationship with Christ is the beginning of all we could want or desire.

Another teaching of the law of attraction is to pay attention to your feelings, follow them, and they will lead you to what you want. This is also contrary to the Word of God. The Bible makes it very clear that our human feelings cannot be trusted. Jeremiah 17:9 says, "The heart is deceitful above all things and desperately wicked; who can know it?" Proverbs 28:26, "He who trusts in his own heart is a fool, but whoever walks wisely will be delivered." Human emotions are not to be trusted. Human emotions often lead to sin. Anger, lust, jealousy, etc. are all emotions that lead us down the wrong path. Humans have a sinful nature. Following our emotions and our mind, is to follow the sinful nature. What we need to pay attention to is the voice of God. John 6:63 says, "It is the Spirit who gives life; the flesh profits nothing. The words that I speak to you are spirit, and they are life." The Enemy, through the law of attraction, pushes individuals towards their feelings. Feelings are promoted as good and trustworthy. Feelings are promoted as aligning with the energy of the universe. Feelings are promoted as the answer to what you need or want. Feelings, in essence, take the place of God and deception takes over.

A third main belief of the law of attraction is "Ask, Believe, Receive". Many proponents of this belief casually equate it to Jesus because in Mark 11:24 Jesus says, "I say to you, whatever things you **ask** when you pray, **believe** that you receive them, and you will **have** them." At first glance, it would seem like this belief is in line with what Jesus taught but again, it is a classic case of taking a verse out of context. In Mark chapter 11, Jesus is speaking to his disciples. They are about the Father's business. Jesus sees a fig tree and is going to pick a fig from it to eat, but there are no figs, so

Jesus curses the fig tree. The next day when the disciples see that the fig tree is withered, they are amazed. Jesus responds by says, "Have faith in God. For assuredly, I say to you, whoever says to this mountain, 'Be removed and be cast into the sea,' and does not doubt in his heart, but believes those things he says will be done, he will have whatever he says. Therefore, I say to you, whatever things you ask when you pray, believe that you will receive them, and you will have them."

The first key to these verses is that the disciples were following Jesus and learning from Him so they could build HIS kingdom does not meet their own needs and desires. In the original language "have faith in God" literally means "have the faith of God." These verses have nothing to do with asking for all the things we want and having them come to us and they most certainly are not about asking the universe to bring forth blessings. The second key to these verses is that they are talking about the miracle power of Jesus and trusting in Him. These verses are all about having faith in God. Having faith in God leads us to His will, His desires, and His thoughts. To say that Jesus is talking about the law of attraction is just another way that the Enemy deceives us.

The fourth main belief of the law of attraction is "your purpose in life is to do what you love and follow your bliss." It is true that we were all born with a purpose. Psalm 139:16 says, "Your eyes saw my substance, being yet unformed. And in Your book, they all were written, the days fashioned for me, when as yet there were none of them." God, our Creator, ordained our purpose before we were even born. We were created as

Law of Attraction (Manifesting)

1 Peter 2:9 tells us "To proclaim the praises of Him who called you out of darkness into His marvelous light." Ephesians 2:10 says, "For we are His workmanship, created in Christ Jesus for good works, which God prepared beforehand that we should walk in them." It is a lie of Satan to buy into our purpose being "to follow our bliss." Again, we find ourselves back at the story or Adam and Eve. Satan encouraged Eve to follow her bliss and ever since, he and his demons have encouraged humans to do just that. To ignore their God ordained purpose and just follow what we THINK is right, what we FEEL is right, and what makes us feel BLISSFUL. This is the lie of the law of attraction.

Believing the four main beliefs of the law of attraction and spending our lives trying to manifest what we desire, puts us on a path to destruction and opens the door for Satanic influence. Ultimately, it is God's purpose that prevails because we were created for Him and only when we accept Christ as our Savior can we begin living our God ordained purpose. Colossians 1:16 tells us, "For by Him all things were created that are in heaven and that are on earth, visible and invisible, whether thrones or dominions or principalities or powers. All things were created through Him and for Him." Proverbs 19:21 says, "There are many plans in a man's heart, Nevertheless the Lord's counsel—that will stand." Psalm 33:11 says, "The counsel of the Lord stands forever, the plans of His heart to all generations." His purpose is what remains true.

The Bible does speak about manifesting but not in the way it is described in the law of attraction. In 2 Corinthians 4:7-10 it says, "But we have this treasure in earthen vessels, that the excellence of the power may be of God and not of us. *We are* hard-pressed on every side, yet not crushed; *we are* perplexed, but not in despair; persecuted, but not forsaken; struck down, but not destroyed—always carrying about in the body the dying of the Lord Jesus, that the life of Jesus also may be manifested in our body." When Paul wrote this, he was focused solely on living his life serving God not using a power of the universe to manifest what he wanted or desired in life. His desire, as should be ours, is to manifest Jesus. Believers are also given the manifestation of the Spirit of God for the benefit of the Body of Christ. 1 Corinthians 12:7 says, "But the manifestation of the Spirit is given to each one for the profit *of all.*" When we manifest Jesus, we are a witness to both unbelievers and our brothers and sisters in Christ.

The only thing that we as humans should manifest is Jesus. Romans 1:18-20 says, "For the wrath of God is revealed from heaven against all ungodliness and unrighteousness of men, who, suppress the truth in unrighteousness, because what may be known of God is manifest in them, for God has shown *it* to them. For since the creation of the world His invisible *attributes* are clearly seen, being understood by the things that are made, *even* His eternal power and Godhead, so that they are without excuse." God designed humans to manifest Him and His glory. He designed the universe to manifest His invisible attributes. This is so people who do not know Him can look at His followers and His creation and see Him, being drawn to Him and finding salvation.

Continuing in Romans 1, we see the description of those who follow beliefs like the law of attraction. Verses 21-23 say, "Because, although they knew God, they did not glorify *Him* as God, nor were thankful, but became futile in their thoughts, and their foolish hearts were darkened. Professing to be wise, they became fools, and changed the glory of the incorruptible God into an image made like corruptible man—and birds and four-footed animals and creeping things." The law of attraction and the idea of manifesting are lies of the enemy. The only law of attraction is the power of the Holy Spirit which attracts us to Christ so that we can receive salvation and manifest Christ and His glory to everybody around us.

Chapter 10:
Astrology

Astrology is a difficult term to define. This is because it encompasses many different aspects of what is referred to as pseudoscience. Pseudoscience is a belief, statement, or practice that claims to be based in science and fact but is not compatible with the scientific method. A Pseudoscience is often given more creditability than it should because it seems to be backed up by science. This is part of what makes Astrology hard to define. For a working definition, we can define Astrology as the study of the influence that distant cosmic objects, usually stars and planets, have on human lives. This influence is then used to predict or "prophesy" about an individual's future, relationships, economic fortune, and life choices. Astrology can come across as a science and in part uses scientific facts such as times and seasons, but in reality, its origins can be found in pagan worship. Pagan worship is worship of a false god. It is idolatry. By masking Astrology as a pseudoscience, its origins and dangers are glossed over or forgotten opening the door to Satan's schemes just as with the New Age Movement.

Satan is a deceiver and as such, he uses these types of tricks to cause something to look innocent or harmless so that we will open the door and invite him in.

God created all cosmic objects, stars, constellations, and planets. They are an important part of God's plan for humanity to see Him as the Creator and for humans to look up to the heavens and see the glory of God. Psalm 19:1 says, "The heavens declare the glory of God; and the firmament shows His handiwork." Genesis 1:16 says, "God made two great lights: the greater light to rule the day, and the lesser light to rule the night. *He made* the stars also." So particular and thoughtful was God about the creation of the stars that He named each one. Psalm 147: 4 says, "He counts the number of the stars; He calls them all by name." Isaiah 40:26 says, "Lift up your eyes on high, and see who has created these *things,* who brings out their host by number; He calls them all by name, By the greatness of His might and the strength of *His* power; Not one is missing."

The estimated number of stars in the heavens is seventy sextillions, which is seventy followed by twenty-one zeros multiplied by seventy followed by twenty-one zeros multiplied by seventy followed by twenty-one zeros and God knows each one by name. Not only was God particular in the names and numbers of the stars He created, but He created them with His very breath. Psalm 33:6 says, "By the word of the Lord the heavens were made, And all the host of them by the breath of His mouth." Not only did God created the vast heavens and uncountable stars with the breath of His mouth, He also commanded them to exist. Isaiah 45:12 says, "I have made the earth, and created man on it.

I—My hands—stretched out the heavens, and all their hosts I have commanded." When he created the heavens, He created the heavens to worship Him. Nehemiah 9:6 says, "You alone *are* the L<small>ORD</small>; You have made heaven, The heaven of heavens, with all their host, The earth and everything on it, the seas and all that is in them, and You preserve them all.

The host of heaven worships You."

When we understand the majesty and creative power that went into creating the stars and the heavens and that they were created by the very breath of God to worship Him, we see why Satan has taken something so Godly and twisted it for his own purposes. It is easy to see the truth of Romans 1:25, "(they) exchanged the truth of God for the lie and worshiped and served the created things rather than the Creator." This is the very tactic of Satan. He, the created being, wanted to be worshipped instead of worshipping the Creator. He is a liar who takes the truth and exchanges it for lies. Lying is his native language. He has taken the beauty of God's creation and removed God from it.

The Babylonians created Astrology. To understand the origin of the Babylonians we can go back to almost the beginning of the Bible itself. In Genesis 10, the descendants of Noah are named, and Nimrod is listed as the founder of the Kingdom of Babel. Immediately after in Genesis 11, we read the story of the Tower of Babel. This is a famous Biblical story as it tells of the people of Babel attempting to build a tower that would reach the heavens. The Lord came down and scattered them giving them different languages. It was the pride of the people, expecting to reach heaven and make a name for themselves, which God was shutting down. It is the same pride that led Satan, when he was an angel in heaven, to try and create a name for himself. God shut him down as well. It is from here, that the Babylonians were developed as a people and a nation. The city of Babylon is mentioned multiple times in the books of the prophets Daniel, Jeremiah, and Isaiah, as well as in the Book or Revelation. It is mentioned due to its sinful nature and culture. It was here that the pagan religion and practice of Astrology began. It then spread to Egypt which at the time was under the control of Greek kings and a Greek form of Astrology was developed.

This leads to the question, what exactly about Astrology makes it a realm and belief system that is controlled by Satan? First, Astrology seeks to understand the human condition and prophesy the future based on the heavens. This is in direct contradiction of God. The human condition can only be understood in light of the Creator. The human condition is one of sinfulness without redemption through Jesus Christ. Secondly, prophecy is a spiritual gift given to believers in Jesus to encourage, exhort, and comfort. I Corinthians 14:3 says, "But he who prophesies speaks edification and exhortation and comfort to men." Using the stars to seek out an understanding of the human condition and to predict or prophetically speak about the future are works of darkness.

Just as with the New Age Movement, it seems innocent enough. Astrology is promoted as entertainment.

No harm no foul. Just grab a newspaper or magazine or download a popular app and read your horoscope. What's the big deal? Read about your Zodiac Sign and how it determines your personality. What is the harm? The harm is that astrology is actually a false religion. It takes the stars, planets, and heavens that were created by God to point to God and attempts to use them to find direction and destiny apart from God. Horoscopes attempt to lead a person into their purpose. Zodiac signs attempt to assign meaning and characteristics to a person's life. Rising moons, rising suns, and astrological signs attempt to replace the voice, purpose, and divine direction of God.

The danger is that after a time, reading horoscopes or determining your fate based on your "sign" is not enough. It is not enough because it does not fill the void and the answers it provides are false. It leads people to seek more and more signs. This can lead to palm reading and tarot card readings and visits to psychics. It takes the place that God desires to have in a person's life. Only God can speak to your purpose, your destiny, your future, your personality, and your characteristics. Only He can answer the questions of life such as what my purpose is, why am I here, how I get out of this situation. Satan, being the Father of Lies, again twists what God created as beautiful, pure, and holy using it to replace God. He uses it to make a person think they do not need God. After all, they have the stars and the reading of their signs and the prophecy of their horoscope. Astrology opens the door to the Satanic realm in the most subtle of ways.

Astrology

Isaiah 47:13-14 is speaking to the fate of the Babylonians who practiced astrology. Isaiah speaks with derision or what we call sarcasm when he says, "Let now the astrologers, the stargazers, *and* the monthly prognosticators stand up and save you from what shall come upon you. Behold, they shall be as stubble. The fire shall burn them; they shall not deliver themselves from the power of the flame; *It shall* not *be* a coal to be warmed by, *nor* a fire to sit before!" Deuteronomy 13:1-3 says, "If there arises among you a prophet or a dreamer of dreams, and he gives you a sign or a wonder, and the sign or the wonder comes to pass, of which he spoke to you, saying, 'Let us go after other gods'—which you have not known—'and let us serve them,' you shall not listen to the words of that prophet or that dreamer of dreams." Individuals who claim to have signs from the heavens, the stars, and other cosmological objects, are inviting you, whether they state it plainly or not, to go after other gods. Do not listen to them. Seek the Lord Jesus Christ and He will provide all the direction, purpose, and divine knowledge you need for your life.

Chapter 11:
Séances and Communicating with the Dead

Most of us have experienced the loss of a loved one. The ability to speak to them after they are dead or "beyond the grave" is something many loved ones left behind would like to have. However, communicating with the dead is not a possibility. When people die, they do not become angels watching over us or ghosts who show up for payback or to check in on our lives. The Bible says in Hebrews 9:27-28, "As it is appointed for men to die once, but after this the judgment, so Christ was offered once to bear the sins of many." The idea of communicating with the dead is found in most cultures but came to the forefront in the nineteenth century when The Fox Sisters held a séance and claimed to be able to see into the spiritual realm. This was also the time when Spiritualism was spreading from Europe to America. Many people came to The Fox Sisters asking for them to contact their dead relatives. There were believers and skeptics alike, but the skepticism did not stop the sisters from becoming famous. Through the next 150 years, more and more "mediums" came to the forefront. Now, it is a common option to seek out a medium or psychic and participate in a séance to communicate with the dead.

Though it may seem like this is a modern idea, the idea of séances and using mediums is not new. In 1 Samuel 28, King Saul is in distress. The Israelite army is going to fight the Philistine army and when King Saul sees how large the Philistine army is, he is in a panic. In the past, he would have gone to the prophet Samuel for advice, but Samuel is dead, and God has removed Himself from King Saul due to his disobedience that was liken to witchcraft. Through dreams and sacred lots, King Saul tries to hear what God says he should do but God is silent. King Saul finds himself without the voice of the prophet and without the voice of God, so he decides he wants to speak to a medium to try and consult Samuel. The problem is that King Saul has already banished all the mediums from Israel. So, he removes his kingly robes and dresses as an ordinary person and goes to En Dor. He goes into the medium's house at night and says, "Please conduct a séance for me, and bring up for me the one I shall name to you" (1 Samuel 28:8). The woman is afraid it is a trap since she knows that King Saul has banned all mediums. She does not yet know she is speaking to King Saul. Saul swears to her by the Lord that nothing bad will happen to her, so she summons a spirit that she says is Samuel. This spirit speaks and tells Saul that because of his disobedience, he and his sons will die the next day and Israel will lose to the Philistines.

The spirit, which the medium claimed to be Samuel, was never seen by Saul. He decided on his own that the spirit was Samuel based on what the medium had said. Mediums are deceptive. Whether they are using demonic powers to cause supernatural things to happen or they are simply deceiving those who seek their counsel, both are orchestrated by the Enemy. Now we see that there are many TV shows that depict being able to speak to the dead. There are popular speakers who travel the world drawing large crowds claiming to be able to speak to the dead. Desperate, hurting people flock to these so-called mediums in a hope that they can talk to their loved one, one last time.

This is a false hope. Mediums and séances cannot give us comfort and peace. They cannot answer questions about our loved ones, and they cannot utter words to dead relatives and friends that we should have uttered before they died. Paul warned of this behavior in 1 Timothy 4:1-2 when he said, "Now the Spirit expressly says that in latter times some will depart from the faith, giving heed to deceiving spirits and doctrines of demons, speaking lies in hypocrisy, having their own conscience seared with a hot iron." Mediums and séances are just another way for Satan to deceive and to promote the supernatural as a way for humans to have their needs met instead of the supernatural being a way for God to speak.

King Saul's legacy is spoken of in 1 Chronicles 10:13, "So Saul died for his unfaithfulness which he had committed against the Lord, because he did not keep the word of the Lord, and also because he consulted a medium for guidance." Remember that it only takes one act, such as going to a medium or a psychic, to open the door to the demonic. Let us live the opposite of King Saul. Let us be faithful to the Lord and keep the word of the Lord and consult only Christ for direction and guidance.

Chapter 12:
Harry Potter

*I*n 1997, J.K. Rowling published the first of a series of books that would come to be known as the Harry Potter Series. The books were later made into blockbuster movies. The books have sold more than 500 million copies worldwide creating an entire Harry Potter franchise. The commercial success of the books and movies cannot be debated, but is the content just a simple story of a child wizard or is the content a celebration and promotion of the occult?

The story follows the main character, Harry Potter, a child wizard, in his journey through wizard training at Hogwarts, a school for young wizards. Through the journey, Harry and his classmates not only learn how to cast spells and fight the dark magic, but they also engage in battles with evil spirits and eventually, Lord Voldemort, the evil wizard who killed Harry's parents when he was an infant.

Throughout the books, Harry learns all about sorcery and witchcraft. He and his cohorts communicate with the dead, deceive their teachers, secretly look in on the thoughts of others, practice divination, and create potions that control the actions of others and even have the power to provide eternal life. Much of the storyline not only shows these practices but also promotes lying to authority, rebellion, and disobedience.

Many people say that the story simply promotes the idea of good vs evil or light vs darkness, a classic theme in literature. They say that Harry Potter is fighting for good and chooses good over evil in various situation. However, this does not mean that the book's "good" outshines the use of witchcraft and divination. The series, promoted to children, makes both witchcraft and divination look fun, exciting, and adventurous. It depicts being a child wizard as a special calling that can change the world.

As sensationalized as the series is, it cannot be ignored that that majority of the books promote witchcraft and divination both of which are forbidden according to the Word of God. Deuteronomy 18:9-12 says, "When you come into the land which the LORD your God is giving you, you shall not learn to follow the abominations of those nations. There shall not be found among you *anyone* who makes his son or his daughter pass through the fire, *or one* who practices witchcraft, *or* a soothsayer, or one who interprets omens, or a sorcerer, or one who conjures spells, or a medium, or a spiritualist, or one who calls up the dead. For all who do these things *are* an abomination to the LORD, and because of these abominations the LORD your God drives them out from before you."

If we look at the specifics of these verses in Deuteronomy 18, we can see the practices that God refers to as abominations. An abomination is something that causes disgust or hatred. It is similar to an atrocity, an obscenity, and an outrage. In other words, the practices described in these verses are practices that God hates. The first thing listed is someone who makes their child walk through the fire. This refers to the pagan rituals of the time where children were literally sacrificed. In Harry Potter, there are circumstances in which children are sent into battles with evil wizards and dark magic knowing that death is an imminent outcome. Their deaths are shown as sacrifices made for the greater good of those around them. They are lauded as heroes. But the reality is, they were children sacrificed to evil.

The second practice listed is the practice of witchcraft. Witchcraft refers to the practice of magic and the use of spells, particularly dark magic. It refers to bewitching someone and controlling their actions with a charm or a spell. The entire premise of the Harry Potter series is the practice of witchcraft. Although it is often portrayed in a fun, harmless way like changing a friend into an animal or candy that comes to life, the events take a very dark turn when the young wizards are found fighting for their lives and casting spells that protect them from the evilest of spirits. The overwhelming darkness that takes over as the series progresses increases the level of witchcraft in which all characters participate. Again, this is portrayed as what is necessary for good to prevail, but the Word of God is clear that any witchcraft is an abomination.

The verses go on to mention types of witches that participate in witchcraft as soothsayers (fortune tellers), those who interpret omens, sorcerers, conjurers of spells, mediums, and those who call up the dead referred to as necromancers. Every one of these types of witches is found in the Harry Potter series. The twist is that the books claim that there are good witches and bad witches, those who use their powers for good and those who use them for evil. The Bible is clear that witches and the practice of witchcraft is not of God and is considered an abomination. There are no good witches who practice witchcraft.

The students at Hogwarts are also exposed to ghosts and demons of all kinds. Some of the ghost died horrible deaths. Moaning Myrtle, a ghost Harry encounters in the bathroom, died by looking into the eyes of a Basilisk who was being controlled by a boy who could talk to evil snakes. Nearly Headless Nick is a ghost who died after being struck multiple times with a dull ax. The students are haunted by Dementors whose job it is to literally suck the souls out of people. The author uses these things to cleverly disguise occultism as a battle between good and evil. Disguising good for evil is a trick of Satan. Remember, 2 Corinthians 11:14 warns us, "For Satan himself transforms himself into an angel of light." We know that when Satan had his conversation with Eve, he makes the bad (eating from the tree) sound and look good.

Since the first Harry Potter book was released and as the franchise has grown over time, there have been Christians who have denounced the series and those who have claimed it is harmless, or even beneficial because it depicts a battle between good and evil. However, there are many classic stories of good vs evil and light vs darkness that do not involve witchcraft and evil practices. The Bible itself is full of stories of how Jesus, the Light of the world has overcome darkness, so why expose us or our children to every form of witchcraft that is contrary to God's Kingdom and is a pagan abomination?

The tolerance of Harry Potter and its portrayal of the occult is one that should not exist within the Body of Christ. Philippians 4:8 says, "Finally, brethren, whatever things are true, whatever things *are* noble, whatever things *are* just, whatever things *are* pure, whatever things *are* lovely, whatever things *are* of good report, if *there is* any virtue and if *there is* anything praiseworthy—meditate on these things." Our meditation should be on the things of God.

Further, Christian parents have the responsibility to raise up their children to understand the supernatural. Deuteronomy 6:6-7 says, "And these words which I command you today shall be in your heart. You shall teach them diligently to your children and shall talk of them when you sit in your house, when you walk by the way, when you lie down, and when you rise up." Teaching, promoting, and participating in the things of God is what Christian parents should be focused on. Exposing children to all forms of witchcraft for the sake of showing a battle between good and evil is irresponsible.

Fans of Harry Potter can purchase wizard robes, wands, and even spell books for themselves or their children. They can "play" wizard speaking seemingly nonsense spells and fight evil Lord Voldemort. We can call this fantasy, sci-fi, imagination, or child's play but what it actually is, is mimicking the occult. Imagine if

Christian adults gathered together and dressed as wizards, speaking spells, and reading imaginary potion books for "fun." It would not be tolerated so why should we allow our children to do so? This causes us to downplay the dangers of the occult and diminish the power of the supernatural.

As believers, we are actively engaged in spiritual warfare and we must do as Ephesians 6:11-17 tells us, "Put on the whole armor of God, that you may be able to stand against the wiles of the devil. For we do not wrestle against flesh and blood, but against principalities, against powers, against the rulers of the darkness of this age, against spiritual hosts of wickedness in the heavenly places. Therefore, take up the whole armor of God, that you may be able to withstand in the evil day, and having done all, to stand. Stand therefore, having girded your waist with truth, having put on the breastplate of righteousness, and having shod your feet with the preparation of the gospel of peace; above all, taking the shield of faith with which, you will be able to quench all the fiery darts of the wicked one. And take the helmet of salvation, and the sword of the Spirit, which is the word of God."

In my case, the ritual I participated in was witchcraft. I was using a spell of sorts to cleanse my house of spirits. I was doing so at the direction of a shaman. Shamans are a type of witch. They are said to have influence over spirts. They practice rituals and divination and healing. In most cultures, shamans, like witches or psychics, claim that they are born with these "gifts," but we know that their power comes from Satan. It is his influence on them that allows these types of powers to be displayed. Really, he is using them for his benefit. He has deceived them so they can deceive others. It brings us back to the book of Genesis when Satan deceived Eve who in turn handed the fruit to Adam and he ate.

We are not playing a game or participating in make believe. Wizards and witches are not fantasy or imaginary. Speaking curses and casting spells are not practices from fiction. Witchcraft is not a story you read to your children before bed. Spiritual warfare is real. As Christians we need to stand firm in our rejection of Harry Potter and other forms of "entertainment" that depict the evils of witchcraft, and we should not allow our children to be desensitized to the supernatural but instead teach them to stand firm, putting on the full armor of God.

Chapter 13:
Conclusion and Poem

When my friend suggested I may have house spirits and that I perform the ritual, he had been deceived and the cycle continued when he passed his deception on to me. My desire in writing this book has been to break the cycle of lies and deception. Telling my story has not been easy. Living my life with the physical and emotional consequences has not been easy. John 8:31-32 says, "If you abide in My word, you are My disciples indeed. And you shall know the truth, and the truth shall make you free." After my fall, as I began to read the Word of God, I longed to find the truth. Since the time I accepted Christ and was baptized, I have abided in His Word, and I am His disciple. I now know the truth and though my body may not be whole as it was before, I am free.

John 8 goes on to say in verse 36, "If the Son makes you free, you will be free indeed." I am indeed free. I am free from the control of the enemy. I am free from my sin. I am free from my confusion. I no longer wander through my life looking for purpose. This is why I have written my story. This is why I have written in detail about the occult, yoga, astrology, witchcraft, and new age because I know how these can all be open doors to demonic influences. We need to acknowledge that the supernatural realm exists and that these are not innocent, harmless things we participate in as part of our culture or as entertainment or because they promote the answers we need. The answer to everything we will ever need is Jesus Christ.

It is my prayer that if you are in any way participating in these occult practices, you will stop immediately as you can see the dangers involved. It is also my prayer that if you have not accepted Christ, you will go back to chapter five (The Lord's church) and re-read the chapter looking for a church of Christ near you. Here are some resources to help you find one: (www.church-of-christ.org) or on Instagram (The Authentic Christian) or on TV/YouTube (Gospel Broadcasting Network / World Video Bible School). I know this book has been spiritually heavy and may seem dark, but it really is about hope, light, love, and salvation. As you have figured out by now, I should be dead. There are so many parts of my story that could have led to my death before my fall and my fall itself should have sealed my fate. However, God in His mercy saved me from physical death and eternal death. He saved my life physically and spiritually. He has brought me hope and joy. He has given me purpose.

Luke 11:33-36 says, "No one, when he has lit a lamp, puts it in a secret place or under a basket, but on a lampstand, that those who come in may see the light. The lamp of the body is the eye. Therefore, when your eye is good, your whole body also is full of light. But

Conclusion and Poem

when your eye is bad, your body also is full of darkness. Therefore, take heed that the light which is in you is not darkness. If then your whole body is full of light, having no part dark, the whole body will be full of light, as when the bright shining of a lamp gives you light." My request to you, my dear readers, is to "take heed that the light which is in you is not darkness."

Surrender your life to Jesus and renounce any ties with the Enemy of your soul. Let your whole body be filled with the light of Jesus that you may shine bright and share His love with others.

God bless you. Amen

> "But as for you, you meant evil against me; *but* God meant it for good, in order to bring it about as *it is* this day, to save many people alive" (Genesis 50:20).

I leave you with this hopeful poem of mine.

The case of Malena Merian

YOUR WORD KEPT ME TOGETHER

I stayed in bed with lots of pain
Dark big monster if you only could walk away

It won't leave this broken paralyzed body
It's like a curse-

I am waiting eagerly for the Word
By His sound he will disappear

A Cockroach in Dover Harbor
Carried away by a Dove

Where I couldn't find you
I couldn't find you-

I travelled the World
To find you at home

In the pages of your Word
I felt finally at home

But no happy end
The devil came in between

He sent his blonde messenger
To feed me lies

Conclusion and Poem

Rotten spirits
Came through my throat

They screamed
I couldn't control

I was destined to fall
But your angel was strong

I was almost a small obituary
Your Word kept me together

My soul was tarnished
But you made it pure

Nine months later
I was born your child

Whole of my body
Delight

Fled the enemy
Finally

Works Cited

(n.d.). Retrieved from Church of Christ: htttp://church-of-christ.org/who

Barnett, J. R. (n.d.). *The Churches of Christ-Who Are These People.*

Disken, E. (2020, September 9). *9 Countries Where Witchcraft is Still Practiced-or Persecuted.* Retrieved from Matador Network: http://matadornetwork.com/read/countries-witchcraft-exists-practiced/

Engelbrecht, R. (n.d.). *New Age Movement & Law of Attraction-Perilous Times Vol 5: Darkness Descends .*

Engelbrecht, R. (n.d.). *Occultism-Choose Life or Death Vol IV.*

Helena Petrovna Blavatsky Quotes. (2021, July 1). Retrieved from Goodreads: http://www.goodreads.com/author/quotes/18295027.Helena_Petrovna_Blavatsky.

Hernandez, V. (2013, November 26). *The Country Where Exorcisms Are On The Rise.* Retrieved from BBC News: http://www.bbc.com/news/magazine-25032305.

Kung, H. (1995). *The Church*. London: Burns & Oates.

Law of Attraction. (2021, April 25). Retrieved from Soigsi Online: http://www.soigsi.online/law-o-f-attraction/

Louise L. Hay Quotes. (2021, July 1). Retrieved from Good Reads: http://www.goodreads.com/author/quotes/74538.Louise_L_Hay.

Pew Research Center. (2020, August 27). Retrieved from Pew Research Center: http://www.pewresearch.org/fact-tank/2018/10/01/new-age-beliefs-common-among-both-religious-and-nonreligious-americans/